SAROJA

Omi Singh

Invincible Publishers

First published in India in 2018

ISBN: 978-93-87328-93-8

Invincible Publishers

G-120, Sushant Lok III, Sector 57, Gurgaon - 122-002

Registered Address: Opposite Kasturba Ashram, Radaur, Haryana - 135-133

Printed at Thomson Press (India) LTD

Dedicated to
All my loved ones, family and friends who encouraged and inspired me to conceptualize the idea of SAROJA and complete the novel.

Acknowledgements

My proof reader, typist, designer, editor, printer and Publishers

Disclaimer

SAROJA is a work of fiction. Names, characters, businesses, places, events, locales, and incidents (except those known in History) are either the products of the author's own imagination or used in a fictitious manner. Any resemblance to actual persons, living or dead, or actual events is purely coincidental.

PART 1

CHAPTER I

BENARAS

In Mahabharata, before the Kurukshetra war begins, Lord Krishna blows the divine conch shell. Similarly, at Varanasi, the priest blows the divine conch shell before each *Ganga aarti*. Pandit Raghupati Chandra Mishras' house in Varanasi (then Benaras) was merely three kilometers from from *Assi Ghat* near the famous *Kaashiwishwanath Temple*.

Pandit ji, as he was affectionately addressed by the locals, was a true nationalist in his thoughts and lifestyle. His wife of six years, Leela Mishra, affectionately called as *panditaeen*, with whom he had gotten married in the summer of 1979 at the age of 24, had given him two children. His four years old son was called Kailash, born on 4th February, 1981, while the younger daughter, only two years old, was named Kanchan, born on 2nd May, 1983. By 1985, he was barely touching thirty. God fearing and down-to-earth by nature, he had only one ambition in life: to become the school principle at

Pt. Dina Nath Malviya Hindi School where he had been employed as the Hindi teacher.

One monsoon night in early July, 1986, after wrapping up dinner and ensuring that both the children were fast asleep, he convinced his wife to make one more attempt for another son. The ever-obedient Indian wife had no courage to refuse the demand of her master husband.

In the month of June, the following year, with the summer season in its last leg and monsoon yet to arrive, the verandah of the Mishra residence witnessed the buzzing activity of woman preparing *papads* and pickles (both mango and red chilli), which was a routine summer occupation for women during this season. It is in fact the customary occupation for most women of the household across India.

On 15th June, 1987, at about 10 AM, the *panditaeen* who was pregnant and expecting the baby to arrive anytime, suddenly felt labour pains and was rushed to the nearby nursing home by the fellow women. Kailash, the elder son, rushed to inform his father that his mother had been taken to the nursing home. Pandit ji immediately rushed to the hospital with his son, where he found the fellow women and Kanchan, his daughter, waiting for him to arrive.

"The delivery will happen in a day or two," one of the women told the pandit ji. For the next few hours at the hospital, he consulted with the doctors and was relieved to know that the baby would indeed arrive in a day or two. He then thanked the women and children gathered there and asked them to leave for home by that afternoon, and so they did. Pandit Mishra remained at the hospital himself till late in the evening that day. Before leaving for home, he requested a nurse there to take extra care of the *panditaaen,* and informed her that he would come back early in the morning the next day.

On June 16th, the next morning, Pandit ji arrived back at the hospital with his children's and few local women's. At about 11 AM, a nurse rushed to him and informed him, "Congratulations! It's a girl."

On hearing that, pandit ji didn't know how to react. His dream of having another son had not come true, but there wasn't much that he could do about it. The fellow women who had gathered there were also not too pleased with the information, of another girl being added to the Mishra household.

"One more girl!" exclaimed one of the women. For Mishra ji's children, however, it wasn't much of an issue. They were happy to know that their little sister had arrived in the world.

"Have you thought of a name for her?" a woman asked pandit ji. He remained quiet. After a few moments, when everyone entered the delivery room where the *panditaeen* lay with the baby girl in a cradle beside her, a woman asked again, "Have you thought of a name for her?"

"Saroja..." answered the *panditaeen* weakly. And thus, Saroja was reluctantly welcomed into the world on 16th June, 1987. In a few days, Leela Mishra was discharged from the hospital and she came back home with her little new born daughter.

Saroja was a very healthy child, had a spark in her eyes and looked just like a doll. Her siblings often address her as *gudiya rani* for this very reason. Although Pandit Mishra felt burdened by the responsibility of raising another girl child, he showers all his love and affection on her. Every day while returning home from school, he would purchase some or the other toys for his little girl. Her siblings were very protective of her and never let anyone else to even come too close to her cradle. Saroja, on the other hand, was always smiling and was adored by all.

Chapter 2

Barabanki

At the beginning of the academic year in June 1988, Pandit Mishra was promoted to the post of the school Principal, but was transferred to the Barabanki branch of Pt. Dina Nath Malviya Hindi School situated in the Nawabganj area. Though Pandit Mishra had never thought of leaving Varanasi in his life, he had to for the sake of taking up that new assignment which he had always dreamed of. His entire family shifted to Barabanki with him and took shelter in the abode provided by the school management. Pandit Mishra let his Varanasi residence out on rent to his own colleague Brijbhushan Sahay, who taught History at the same school in Varanasi.

Barabanki is known as the entrance to Purvanchal. It comes under the Faizabad district and is barely a forty minutes' drive from Lucknow. The city is popular for its Mahadev temple and Dewa – the pilgrimage town situated just 12 kilometers from Barabanki–the birth place of Hazi Waris Ali Shah.

He was born to the *Hussaini Syeds* in the 19th century. He grew up to be a *sufi* saint and influenced the lives of many generations with his message of universal love and humanity. He was regarded in high esteem by both Hindus and Muslims.

Barabanki was also famous for the *Parijaat* tree- which was regarded as very sacred. Many folklores surround the origin of this tree. Some say that Arjuna of the Mahabharata brought this tree down from the heavens, while others believe that the tree was brought by Lord Krishna for his beloved queen Satyabhama. Whether one believed in these sayings or not, it is true that the tree is rare and has a very ancient background. It is mentioned in the Harivansh Puraan that Parijaat is a type of '*Kalpvraksh*'. This sacred tree of Parijaat situated in the Kintoor village of Barabanki, holds a very special place in the world. It is known as Adansonia Digitata in botanical terms and comes under a special category of trees. It does not produce either fruits or seeds, neither can another tree of such kind be grown by cutting its branch and planting it. It is one of its kind, a unisex male tree. Botanists believe that there is no such tree anywhere else in the world.

Inside the school premises, in vicinity of the head master Pandit Mishra's new residence, there lived the family of Mr. Ramesh Singh. He was a *thakur,* the Vice Principle, as well as the mathematics teacher at the same school. He had been provided residence there by the school management too. Thakur Ramesh Singh (as he preferred to be addressed) and his wife, Mamata Singh, had only a son of two years, named Brijesh Singh, born on 11th October 1986. Married for three years, they had both come from influential Rajput families from the Sultanpur district of Uttar Pradesh. In the caste dominated state of U.P., the Thakurs and the Brahmins jointly played a very vital role in the politics and governance of the state.

Head Master Pandit Raghupati Chandra Mishra soon became friends with his colleague, Thakur Ramesh Singh. In the Mandal and Kamandal era of politics, it was a friendship of convenience for both of them, since the rest of the teachers were either from the *kayastha* or *baniya* community, while the administrative and other school staff comprised largely of Yadavs or other lower castes. Besides, most of the other teachers lived at their personal residences in the surrounding locality.

Over the next five years, children from the Mishra and Singh households grew up together and became childhood buddies. Saroja and Brijesh, being of the same age, often played together. On the birthday of each kid, the families would visit the temple in a traditional way to pray for a better future for the kid and the family.

Through these five years, history was being made in the political and administrative spheres of the country. Right-wing leader L.K. Advani took the

Rath Yatra in support of building the Ram Temple at Ayodhya, where the Babari Masjid stood; India lost its charming Prime Minister Rajeev Gandhi in an assassination attempt on 21st May, 1991; Government of India, led by the new Prime Minister V.P. Singh, implemented the Mandal Commission, establishing reservations for backward and other backward classes, leading up to an all India protest against it. Both these events took place in the early 1990's.

Back in Barabanki, young Kailash had grown overprotective of Saroja. He would often ask Brijesh to leave when she was fast sleep. "*Gudiya* is sleeping…you should go sleep too," Kailash would often say when he saw a toddler Brijesh coming near her. Kanchan would play with her dolls with Saroja, while Pandit Mishra and his wife showered all their love and affection over their children. The heartbreak and remorse of having a second girl child had vanished a long time ago.

Kailash and Kanchan had been put in the same school where Pandit Mishra was the Principle. Kailash was in the 6th standard then, while Kanchan was in 4th. Both the siblings would leave the house at 7 AM each morning and returned in the afternoon, eager to spend the rest of the day with their beloved baby sister.

Once, a mosquito bit Saroja while she was sleep. When she woke up crying, Kailash fought with his parents and threatened them, "If anything happens to my doll, I am telling you I won't spare anyone." This compelled them to purchase a mosquito repellent as well as a net to protect their little toddler. These children were equally fond of Brijesh, while for Thakur Ramesh Singh and Mamata, they were like their own children from an extended family.

Brijesh, now 6 years old, was studying in 2nd standard at Anand Bhawan, a convent school in Barabanki.

"We need to start sending *gudiya* to school this year," Leela Mishra told her husband Pandit Mishra.

"Alright, we will get her enrolled in our school," said Pandit Mishra.

"No, she will go to an English medium school, Mishra ji. I want her to get enrolled in the same school as Brijesh," she insisted.

"Alright," said Pandit Mishra in a resigned manner.

Come June 1992, Saroja was admitted to Anand Bhavan Convent School. It soon became a regular routine for Saroja and Brijesh to go to school together in the same school bus, share their tiffins together, play together and even study together at times.

The year 1992 is remembered best for two things in the country. On every street and every corner, one could find people talking about–one, Sachin Tendulkar's batting, and the other, the *Ram*

Janmabhoomi Movement. People expected Sachin Tendulkar to score a century in every match he played, while the majority of Hindu groups wanted a Ram Temple to be built in place of the Babari Masjid at Ayodhya, which was only a two hour's drive from Barabanki.

On 6th of December, 1992, the Babari Masjid was demolished by Right-wing political groups and *kar-sevaks*, leading to country wide riots amongst the Hindus and the Muslims. More than 2000 people were killed in the riot affected areas across India, but Barabanki, by and large, was at peace, despite having a sizeable Muslim population. The Mishras and the Singhs looked after each other in those difficult times. Their Muslim neighbours were kind and supportive to not aggravate the situation, rather contributed in the maintenance of peace and harmony.

Maulana Shiraj Ahmed appealed to the city's Muslim groups to maintain the peace and harmony of their town. He even met with Pandit Mishra and Thakur Ramesh Singh to assure them that communal tension will be prevented at all costs, and the two reciprocated the same sentiment. As promised, no communal tension was fed to flare up and the people of Barabanki cautiously welcomed the New Year on the eve of 31st December, 1993. With the passage of time, all tension disappeared and the festivals of Sankranti, Holi, Eid and Diwali were celebrated with great enthusiasm, zeal and passion.

On 15th August, 1994, after all the Independence Day rituals had been performed at school, the Mishra clan decided to go watch the movie '*Hum Aapke Hain Kaun*' at a local cinema hall. It was perhaps after years that Mr. and Mrs. Mishra had planned to go watch a movie. This Salman Khan and Madhuri Dixit starrer was receiving accolades all over the country and had been an instant hit. They asked Thakur Ramesh Singh to accompany them with his family as well. He agreed, albeit reluctantly, and all of them decided to go together for the evening show.

In those days, going to the cinema hall for a movie was an event in itself. Everyone took their time to dress up and managed to reach the hall just in time. Thakur Ramesh Singh had already gotten them good tickets beforehand, using his position of influence as the vice principle of the school. Hiring the three-wheeler *rikshaws*, the families reached the venue, since neither had any personal means of transport.

"It was such a good film, wasn't it?" said Leela Mishra to Mamata Singh on their way back home after the show.

"Yes, I liked it very much, sis," she replied.

"I liked Salman," said Kailash.

"Me too, I liked him very much," chimed in Brijesh.

Kanchan and Saroja were too occupied with their ice-creams to talk, while Mr. Mishra and Mr. Singh were engaged in a deep conversation about the school and its expansion plans.

"When I grow up, I shall marry Brijesh," Saroja said suddenly in her stammering voice, and everyone started laughing.

"No, you idiot. I will marry Madhuri Dixit," Brijesh replied in hurry.

Children, in their innocence, say a lot many things, unaware that they might just come true if dictated so by their destiny. Neither Mr. and Mrs. Mishra nor Mr. and Mrs. Singh knew what the fate of these two children, Saroja and Brijesh, held for them. Or rather, for all their children.

It was late in the night when they reached home. The God of rain showered the town of Barabanki with his generosity that night. Saroja and Brijesh were fast sleep in their respective homes, with dreams in their eyes. For the next ten years, life moved in with peace and prosperity for the Mishra and Singh households.

Their children grew up to welcome prosperous futures. Kailash, now an engineering graduate, had secured admission at the coveted IIM–A; Kanchan was pursuing her post-graduation in mass-communication from Delhi University, Saroja was in her first year of B.A. at Jawahar Lal P.G. College, while Brijesh was in the last year of his graduation at the same college and stream as Saroja. He had diligently been preparing for the UPSC examination as well. Being in the same college, Brijesh and Saroja interacted on a daily basis and continued to share their lunch boxes and time roaming around the campus. They adored each other.

Whether it was love blossoming between them, or just infatuation, or perhaps something else entirely, they didn't know. It was, however, a unique relationship shared between a Brahmin girl and a Rajput boy.

Chapter 3

Parijaat

Parijaat flowers/trees are found in Kintoor village, located in the Sirauli Gauspur Tehsil of Barabanki district in Uttar Pradesh, India. It is situated about four kilometers away from the sub district headquarters at Sirauli Gauspur, and 32 kilometers away from the district headquarters at Barabanki.

Saroja was mesmerized with the flower when Brijesh first gave it to her. He had taken her to Kintoor on his new bicycle on the eve of his birthday on 11th October, 2004.

"You are so cheap. Are you not going to treat me with ice-cream on your birthday?"she asked.

"I will," Brijesh replied.

"Anyway, many happy returns of the day," she greeted him cheerfully. "These flowers are too beautiful, aren't they, Brijesh?" she asked.

"Yes, but not as beautiful as you," he replied.

Saroja smiled and looked at him, but didn't say anything. "What are these flowers called?"she asked after a while.

"These are the parijaat flowers," he replied.

"Let's go home now," she requested. He agreed and turned around to go homeward. On their return journey, they remained quiet for the most part. Finally, Brijesh broke the silence between them by starting to tell her about the parijaat flowers.

"Parijaat flowers have four to eight petals, arranged in a pinwheel pattern above a vibrant orange tube. They are highly fragrant and bloom at night to spread their intensely sweet floral aroma in their surroundings. These flowers blossom from August to December. Their tree is sometimes called the *tree of sorrow* because the flowers wilt and drop during daytime.

On reaching their neighbourhood, Saroja got down a few meters ahead of her house near a peepul tree. It was around 6 PM in the evening, and the weather had grown considerably chilly.

"Will you not give me my birthday gift?" Brijesh asked her. She took out a Cadbury's chocolate bar and handed it to him.

"Thanks," he said while receiving it.

"What about my gift?" she asked him.

He grabbed her hand and pulled her close to himself.

"Ouch" she yelped. "Brijesh, it's hurting my wrist. What is all this?"

Brijesh simply looked deep into her eyes while she complained, gave a smile and planted his lips on hers. His arms were wrapped tightly around her, hugged her close.

"Umm..." she could not utter a word till he finally released her lips from under his. "Brijesh! You idiot!" she yelled in anger and gave him a tight slap on his right cheek. "You are disgusting," she said at the edge of tears and then ran away.

Brijesh realized that if he did not stop her soon, she might spill it all to her parents, which would only complicate the issue. He immediately ran after her. Catching up to her before she could enter the compound where their houses were, he asked for her forgiveness with a promise to never repeat the mistake.

Saroja was still shocked. Giving him an angry look, she stormed inside and went straight to her room. Her parents sensed something odd in her behaviour.

"What happened, Saroja?"asked her mother, Leela Mishra.

"Nothing, mom. It's just a little headache. I will come out once I feel better," she answered.

Both her parents as well as Brijesh now felt relieved. He had heard this conversation while standing at a corner near the Mishras' residence.

When Pandit Mishra saw him, he said, "Come inside, my son."

"Uncle, today is my birthday. I have come to seek your blessings," he said and bowed down to touch his feet. Saroja walked out of her room just then.

"God bless you, son," said Mr. and Mrs. Mishra, resting their palms over his head. "Saroja, will you not wish Brijesh? It is his birthday today," Mrs. Mishra said to Saroja. She looked at him coldly and wished him, to which he reverted with a thanks.

"Sit down for some time, son," Pandit Mishra insisted.

"No, uncle. I have to go to the temple, so I will have to leave now. I will bring ice cream for you later," he said while looking at Saroja.

"You don't have to, I am not in the mood," she replied.

"Alright," he said and left their house. He didn't actually go to any temple. Instead, he went straight to his house and acted as if nothing had happened.

Thereafter, Saroja never went out with Brijesh, nor did she share her tiffin with him at college. They started behaving as only acquaintances, and not like the childhood buddies that they were. Brijesh didn't know how to react to this situation. He kept thinking about the relationship they had shared, and what had it been if not love. He never got an answer for it. He never visited the Kintoor village again either, for the parijaat tree had indeed become the tree of sadness for him.

However, he didn't know that Saroja had blossomed a special place for parijaat in her heart and she would often go to Kintoor to see them. Only this time, she would go with Kabir Prajapati – the son of a potter, occupying a lower rung in the cast dynamics of U.P.

Kabir, as he was fondly called by his friends, was known for his dare-devilry and close associations with the political establishment at Barabanki. He was rash, arrogant, extremely stubborn, and could go to any extent to achieve what he desired.

Kabir had seen Saroja at the railway station a few days before, where she had gone to receive her sister, Kanchan. She had come from Delhi on the 22nd of October on the day of Dussehra. Kabir had been there to receive some politician who was arriving to grace some function on the auspicious festival. Saroja didn't know Kabir then, and saw him for the first time standing just behind Kanchan. For a fraction of a second, their eyes had met and it was love at first sight for both of them. Kabir had sensed that much in her eyes as well.

He followed Saroja from there and managed to introduce himself to her. "I am Kabir...Kabir Prajapati, from right here in Barabanki," he said while looking at Saroja.

"She didn't know how to react, so she simply looked at Kanchan and said, "Let's go, sister." Both of them proceed out of the railway station thereafter. Kabir went after her and handed her his visiting card, gesturing at her to call him on his number.

Though a little scared, Saroja admired his confidence and guts. She nodded at him and turned back to Kanchan, who had been so busy with managing her luggage that she didn't even notice the little silent conversation that had been shared between Kabir and Saroja. They called for a taxi and zoomed off to their house.

Saroja managed to call Kabir from a PCO that same evening and they agreed to meet the next day at Kintoor village under the parijaat tree. It soon became a regular practice for both of them to visit Kintoor– the home of parijaat flowers– to meet each other.

"I am very fond of these flowers," she would tell Kabir.

"And I am very fond of you," Kabir would reply. Saroja would then blush on hearing it.

On 12th November, 2004, it was a Friday as well as the day of Diwali. Saroja somehow managed to escape from home on the pretext of going to the market, and came to Kintoor with Kabir. She was wearing a white salwar kameez with a blue dupatta around her neck and hanging behind her back. Her long hair was pulled to one side over her right shoulder and cascaded down the right side of her curvy frame. The blue *bindi* added to her charm and made her look even prettier. On her left side, Kabir could see the cream coloured brassiere that she had on underneath the light kameez, that matched with the colour of her skin below the neck.

The mischievous and playful Kabir picked up a flower from the ground and threw it at her. Tumbling down her upper chest, it fell in to her bra. Her fair cheeks turned red and her heartbeat increased. She controlled herself and asked him, "*Ye kya hai, Kabir?*"

"*Tum kaho toh nikal du waha se*," he said with a naughty smile. She didn't say anything. Kabir came a little closer to her, looked into her eyes and pushed her against the parijaat tree. She was now standing below the tree, her back touching the trunk. Both her hands were free, but she didn't resist Kabir. He drew closer to her and put his right hand over her left breast. Her heartbeat increased further. She didn't utter a word of resistance. A few parijaat leaves were falling now and then from the branches of the tree. He put his finger inside her bra, touching her soft curves and removed the stray petal from between them, but not before giving her nipples a squeeze.

"Ouch! Someone will see," she warned Kabir.

"No one is around," he said and continued with his act of squeezing both her breasts, but with a little more force this time.

Ouchhh! Kabir, it's hurting," she reacted. He remained silent, then put his lips on hers and smooched her passionately.

It was a special Diwali for both of them. In another hour, they returned to their respective houses. Before parting, they hugged each other and exchanged Diwali greetings.

For another year, Kabir and Saroja continued their romance in the vicinity of Kintoor village. They would often lie down beneath the parijaat tree for hours and look up at its divine flowers.

The tree itself is not without its share of tales which suggest its romantic origin. Close to the heart of lovers is the take of *Princess Parijaataka*, who was in love with the Sun. She tried a lot to win the heart of the Sun, but when he rejected her, she committed suicide and a tree sprung from her ashes. Unable to stand the sight of her lover still, the tree flowers only at night and sheds them all like tear drops before the sun rises each morning. That is how the tree is, even today! To this day, it holds the distinction of being the only tree whose flowers can be picked from the earth and still be offered to the Gods. These white flowers arranged in a pinwheel pattern around an orange stem spread their mellow fragrance in the air at night.

One day, Kabir told Saroja, "We shall come here in the morning to collect these flowers. They blossom at night and drop down before sunrise in the morning. It looks mesmerizing when you see them spread on the ground. It seems as if the moon has descended to lay on the ground with an orange *bindi* on its forehead."

"It'll be difficult for me to leave so early in the morning, but I will try," she replied. Saroja lived up to her promise and managed to come to Kintoor every morning on some or the other pretext. She would often convince her parents by saying that she needed to leave early to go to the library and reading the literature of eminent writers, as she never got the time to read once her lectures began at college.

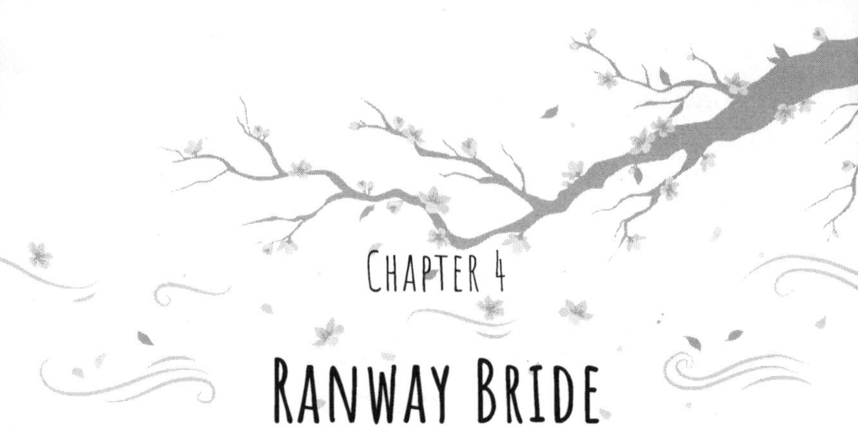

Chapter 4

Ranway Bride

In the beginning of 2006, both Kabir and Saroja found themselves madly in love with each other, despite knowing well enough that their relationship would not be approved of by their families due to the difference in their cast. The Mishra clan could never even think of Saroja marrying a lower caste Kurmi boy. Also, both her siblings were still unmarried and there was no question of her getting married before them. Kabir, on the other hand, was the only son in the Parjapati family, so they wanted him to marry and settle down at the earliest and look after their flourishing pottery business thereafter, which had achieved great success due to Kabir's political connections.

Brijesh, upon completing his graduation, had enrolled for a post-graduation in political science. He was in the second year of his post graduate course and had managed to clear the UPSC preliminary exam as well. In fact, he was waiting for result for mains which he had attempted a while ago.

A day before holi, Saroja met Brijesh and told him that she never considered him to be her boyfriend. It had just been a very special relationship between them where she felt protected in his company. This was all until the day he had kissed her, which destroyed her trust in him. Still, she considered him her best friend, a childhood friend, who would stand by her in her difficult times. She never disclosed her relationship with Kabir to him.

With a grim face, Brijesh told her that he loved her single-mindedly and perhaps hadn't realized that it was only one-sided. "When you were a child, you'd always say that you would marry Brijesh. I guess I was wrong. Forgive me," he said with tears in his eyes. Brijesh indeed loved Saroja, but Saroja never had any feeling for him and considered him no more than a very close childhood friend.

It was her last year of college and she put in all the extra effort in her studies to secure good marks. Kabir had not studied beyond the 12th standard, but he encouraged Saroja in the preparation of her exams which were scheduled to be held in April. He even curtailed their meetings so that she would concentrate wholly on her exams.

By the end of May, Kailash had passed out of IIM and had secured a placement at a multi-national consulting firm in Gurgaon as a finance analyst. Kanchan finished her mass-com and was offered a journalist's position at a news channel based out of Noida. Brijesh had successfully cleared the UPSC mains and was awaiting results of the interview. Saroja was done with her exams too and was waiting for her results.

All the siblings had come for a small vacation at Barabanki before departing to take on their respective careers. Saroja's birthday was also nearing, so her siblings decided to gift her a scooty from whatever savings they had. In all these days, when her siblings had come home, she could barely find the time to meet Kabir. The entire Mishra and Singh clans would gather together, barring Brijesh and Saroja. Brijesh often excused himself on some pretext or another, while Saroja barely got out of her room to be with them. She was missing her beloved Kabir whom she could not meet. Even in the days of mobile phones and internet chat messengers, they were both helpless. Saroja had neither a cell phone nor any internet connectivity at home. Though Kabir had a cell phone, he wasn't into internet chatting much, so he didn't really care for internet connectivity at his end.

On 16th June, at seven in the morning, Saroja rushed out of her house. When Kailash asked where she was going so early in the morning, she replied, "Not far, just to the temple."

"Alright and listen, happy birthday!"

"Thanks, brother," she said and hurriedly disappeared out of his sight. She made her way straight to Kintoor, to the same place beneath the same parijaat tree where she saw Kabir waiting for her.

"You have taken my life, it has been over a month since you last met me. I, like an idiot, come here every morning and wait for you, hoping that you will come, but you never did. I can't imagine my life without you, not even my death. I didn't know whether I should leave or die…" Kabir said with a choked voice and tears in his eyes. Saroja just hugged him tight and explained her problem to him.

"Happy birthday," he said and gifted her a Nokia 3310 with a sim card already installed and instructed her to call him with the same.

"Thank you. By the way, what is your birth date?" she asked Kabir.

"29th February, 1984," he replied.

"Does that mean you celebrate your birthday only once in every four years?" she asked and stared laughing. "Let's go now. I have to leave. Everyone must be waiting for me at home," she said and turned around, only to find Brijesh standing in front of them.

Before Kabir could react, she asked Brijesh, "What are you doing here?"

"Forget about me. You tell me what you are doing with this man? Who is he?" Brijesh asked. "I followed you all the way here when I saw you leaving early in the morning for Kintoor," he continued.

"Look Brijesh, this is Kabir... Kabir Prajapati," she replied.

"Kabir Prajapati," he repeated while looking at Kabir, and drew closer to Saroja.

"Since when has it been going on?" he asked Saroja.

"What are you concerned?" Kabir finally raised his voice at Brijesh.

"We don't talk to lower caste people," Brijesh replied, ignoring Kabir.

Kabir could not control his anger and gave Brijesh a tight slap on his right cheek. It had come with such force that he fell down to the ground. Kabir gave him a hand and said, "We belong to the caste that makes pots from mud. We give earth the shape of statues which you upper caste people keep in your temples. You don't realize at that time that we are from a lower caste, do you?" Kabir pulled him up and continued. "Listen brother, you may be whatever to Saroja, I don't care. I only know one thing, which is that I love her more than my own life."

Saroja was silent. Brijesh smiled and said, "I have loved Saroja since the time when you were not even there in her life."

Kabir was shocked and looked at Saroja for an answer.

"No no," she uttered in haste, but Brijesh cut her short and said, "It's just that she never loved me back."

Both Saroja and Kabir were relieved to hear it. Brijesh apologized to Kabir for his remark and left the place with an assurance to them that he would neither come in between them, nor inform any of the family members of their relationship. In another ten minutes, Brijesh disappeared. Saroja and Kabir returned to their respective houses too.

That evening, Saroja was gifted a scooty by Kailash and everyone from the Mishra and Singh families celebrated her birthday together. Brijesh wished her too, but soon requested to be excused on account of not feeling very well.

A few days thereafter, Saroja's siblings moved out of Barabanki for their respective future engagements and gave her their contact details and cell phone numbers. Brijesh successfully cleared the UPSC exam and was selected for the IAS. He left Barabanki for his training at Mussoorie. Saroja cleared her graduation with first class and was confused as to what she should do thereafter, since she didn't want to move out of Barabanki for the obvious reason that Kabir, her beloved, couldn't move out of his home town.

As the God of rain showered his blessings over the city come monsoon, Kabir and Saroja showered love over each other whenever they got the time. Kabir had managed to rent out a house where the two often met to satisfy their uncontrolled temptations of physical love. In one such act of passion, Kabir unintentionally forgot to wear protection. Saroja felt scared and told Kabir, “If I get pregnant, I won’t abort the child, I am telling you.”

“My love, you won’t need to abort. We shall elope and get married,” Kabir replied.

A month after 24th July, Saroja’s apprehensions came true. Her menstrual cycle got missed. She texted Kabir on his cell phone, “I am pregnant. What do we do now?”

Kabir asked her to meet him at the same room that evening. As planned, she met him there and he suggested to her that they elope and get married, since he had already arranged for it all.

Kabir requested her to meet him in Kintoor under that same Parijaat tree the next morning, 25th July, from where he would pick her up and take her to Bareilly. As planned, Kabir frisked her away from Kintoor in a Maruti Gipsy and drove her to the Mankameswar Mahadev Temple where they formally got married in the presence of Lord Shiva. Kabir had arranged for a local priest who conducted the marriage ceremony in the presence of two of Kabir’s trusted lieutenants Bunty Verma and Munna

Jaiswal. Soon after the temple marriage ceremony got over, Kabir hugged them both and said goodbye, then left with his newly wedded wife.

The previous night, while packing her bags with all her relevant things and documents, Saroja had ensured that she had her parents' and siblings' contact details safely stored in her cell phone. She had also left a hand-written note on her study table, disclosing everything and her intention to spend the rest of her life with Kabir. In the note, she stated that it was a difficult decision for her to make, but had no other option. Though she loved her family, they would not have approved of her relationship with Kabir, so she sought their blessings through the letter and pleaded for them to forgive her, if possible.

Leela Mishra was the first one to know about the same when she entered Saroja's room that day. On reading the letter, she panicked and screamed, "Listennn! See what Saroja has done." With the note in her hand, she ran towards pandit Mishra who was getting ready to go to school. He read the note and fainted. Leela Mishra didn't know how to react. She ran straight to Thakur Ramesh Singh to ask for his help and the entire Singh family reached Pandit Mishra's house within a few minutes. Pandit Mishra regained his consciousness in some time and asked for Saroja. Thakur Ramesh managed to console him and hurriedly informed Kailash and Kanchan of all that had transpired in their absence. They immediately rushed back to Barabanki. Whether it was deliberate or unmindful of Thakur Ramesh Singh, it cannot be determined, but he didn't inform Brijesh of anything.

On her way to Bareilly, Saroja constantly thought of her parents and siblings. She figured that they must have come to know of everything by that time. She looked into Kabir's eyes, who just gave her a smile and the assurance that everything would be alright in a few days. Kabir had sounded his intention to his parents, with the request to not disclose it to anyone.

Kailash and Kanchan arrived at Barabanki within two days. They could not believe that Saroja had run away with some lower caste boy. So helpless was their condition that they could not even complain to the local police station about the incident, thinking of the embracement it would bring them. Moreover, Saroja was an adult who had run away of her own will.

Kailash managed to get the details of Kabir's parents somehow and went to their residence with his father and Thakur Ramesh Singh to meet them. Kailash tried to reason with them, saying that what Kabir had done wasn't right and if they knew of their whereabouts, they should inform them. Kabir's parents understood the plight of pandit Mishra, but they pleaded their ignorance with folded hands.

Almost two weeks went by, but Saroja and Kabir were still untraceable. Finally, the Mishra family conceded to what fate had planned for them. Kailash and Kanchan left their hometown again to go back to their respective workplaces, leaving behind their embarrassed and aging parents who were putting up a brave face. Pandit Mishra had no option but to keep everything low profile, since he was the upholder of the Principal's position at school and could not have taken an irrational attitude of coming in the way of two adults from different caste marrying each other, even if it was against his wish. Through this ordeal, Thakur Ramesh Singh and his family stood by them like a rock. It was only after Kailash and Kanchan had left that they disclosed the entire incident to Brijesh in one of their conversations over the phone. Brijesh reacted as if he didn't know anything about Saroja and Kabir. Kailash and Kanchan kept in regular touch with their parents and the Singh family. Brijesh regularly spoke to Mr. and Mrs. Mishra, as well as to Kailash and Kanchan too. He was undergoing IAS training at Mussoorie then.

At the Mishras' abode, Saroja's scooty still remained parked outside the house. Whenever her parents would see the scooty, their eyes turned wet. "What has *gudiya* done? I never expected such a thing from her. She has always been so mature and understanding," Leela would tell Pandit Mishra who would just listened to it and keep quite. Thakur Ramesh Singh and Mamata Singh often spent their time with the Mishras. The ageing parents from both the families would share all their grief with each other. “No grief is worse than losing your child,” Leela would often say, but it was their fate and they had to accept it, come what may.

Chapter 5

Bareilly

Since coming to the city on 25th July, 2006, Kabir and Saroja lived in rented house in the Bareilly cantt. area. After almost two months since their arrival, Kabir somehow managed to start earning as a social worker through the political contacts from his Barabanki days. Saroja was almost three months' pregnant by then. She had carried all her educational and other relevant testimonials from her home, and enrolled for a post-graduation in English Literature at Bareilly College.

Bareilly is also known by the name of '*Nath Nagri*' (for the four Shiva temples located in the four corners of the region – *DhopeshwarNath*, *MadniNath*, *AlakhaNath* and *Trivati Nath*) WW, *Ala Hazrat*, *ShahSharafatMiyan* and *KhankaheNiyazia* (derived from the famous Muslim Mausoleums), *Zarinagari,* and historically as Sanjashya (where the Buddha descended from Tushita to the Earth). The city is a centre for furniture manufacturing and trade in cotton, cereal and sugar.

After a few months of struggle, Kabir started his own business of furniture trade for a steady income, and as fate would have it, he achieved great success with his hard work and dedication in a very short period of time. They celebrated Dussehra and Diwali, albeit without their loved ones from their home town, and the year 2006 drew to a close.

The new year of 2007 brought Kabir and Saroja great news as Kabir finally opened his furniture store in the Bareilly market and named it 'Saroja Furnitures' after his wife. He had acquired the space on rent to start the store. Gradually, it turned out to be a successful venture for him and gave him financial stability. He showered all his love on Saroja and waited eagerly to welcome his bundle of joy in the coming months. Saroja was happy in the company of Kabir, but she missed her siblings and parents immensely. She thought of calling them many a times, but was too scared to act on it.

In April 2007, Saroja appeared for her first year's PG exams, while still carrying the baby. The exams got over by the month's end.

Come May 27th, 2007, she delivered a baby girl at a local nursing home. Kabir took his little angel in his arms and kissed her forehead. Saroja held his hand and smiled. "Thank you for giving me this little angel," said Kabir. Saroja looked at her little daughter and smiled. Kabir informed his parents of the new arrival by his cell phone, but Saroja didn't call her family back home. She knew that her family wouldn't accept Kabir or her daughter who was later named *Ria*.

On Saroja's birthday, Kabir gifted her a brand-new cellphone with a new sim card installed, and made sure that it had all the contact numbers from Barabanki, including her parents and siblings and his own parents, stored in it. Since only a few days had passed post the delivery of their child, Saroja and Kabir didn't indulge in any passions on her birthday. Kabir celebrated her birthday with a dinner at a well-known restaurant in the city.

Saroja cleared her first year of PG and enrolled for the second year. She would attend the morning lectures and return home by 10.30 AM. Till then, Kabir would take care of Ria. Once Saroja was back, he would leave for his furniture store in the Maruti gypsy which he had brought from his home town. This was the daily routine for them.

On 21st October, 2007, it was a Sunday and the day of Dussehra too. Kabir and Saroja conducted the *pooja* at home and then at the furniture store in the evening. They decided to take a two days' tour of Agra the coming Friday. "Please complete your packing properly and well in time," Kabir told Saroja.

"Yes," she replied and took the rest four days out for the packing.

On 26th October, 2007, they left for Agra with their new born at about 10 P.M. Kabir was at the wheel of his Maruti Gypsy, while Saroja sat behind with Ria.

"Hi Dad, Saroja and I are leaving for Agra and will stay there for two or three days. Ria is also with us," Kabir informed his father over his cell phone. In another 45 minutes, they crossed Binawar, 30 minutes before reaching the Budaun district, where a speeding truck appeared in front of their car. Its headlight flashed directly in Kabir's face through the Gypsy's windscreen. He was blinded for a second and blinked his eyes, losing control of the wheel. Before he could make sense of what was happening, the car smashed into the truck coming onwards. The few vehicles following behind the truck and the Gypsy tried to control their speed and pushed down their breaks to avoid a collision. They were successful, but the Maruti Gypsy kept beeping as Kabir's head had smashed against the wheel and there was blood all over it.

Saroja and Ria fell out of the right side of the vehicle and lay unconscious. Villagers from the nearby settlements gathered around. The truck driver and his companion ran away, while the other commuters on the road stopped to help. An ambulance was called along with the local police. The three injured bodies were immediately taken to the Budaun District Hospital. Kabir was declared dead on arrival, while Saroja and Ria were given initial treatment.

The Binawar police station informed the district's SSP office about the accident, which subsequently updated the SDM of Budaun. Brijesh Singh, whose first posting as an SDM was at Budaun, visited the district hospital the next morning at 8 AM. The hospital in-charge informed him about the incident and took him to the bodies that had been brought in the previous night. When he saw them, he was shocked to recognize the familiar faces. He immediately knew that the dead person was Kabir, and the unconscious female was Saroja. He didn't know who the small baby was, but the doctors informed him that she probably was the daughter of the female, while the deceased seemed to be her husband.

"He was indeed her husband," Brijesh told them. "K...k...Kabir is his name. I know them from my hometown, Barabanki," he continued, while the doctors listened diligently. Brijesh instructed the hospital to shift the female and the baby girl to the Bareilly District Hospital in Civil Lines, as it was better equipped with facilities for treatment. He further instructed them to keep the dead body at the morgue.

Brijesh then informed Saroja's parents and siblings of all this, who immediately rushed to Bareilly upon hearing the news. He also requested the SSP at Budaun to inform Kabir's family of his death. The police was immediately put on the job to trace out Kabir's father's number from the cellphone recovered from Saroja, and inform him of the accident. Kabir's father was shocked to hear about the demise of his only son. He enquired about Saroja and Ria, to which he was updated on their whereabouts. He immediately proceeded to Budaun to collect the dead body of his only son.

Back at the Bareilly District Hospital, Saroja and Ria were treated well and were fortunately drawn out of the clutches of danger. Except for a few injuries on Saroja's head and some scratches on Ria's legs, they had been spared any fatal wounds. Saroja wasn't aware of Kabir's death still. When she opened her eyes and saw her parents and siblings in front of her, she asked for Kabir and Ria.

"Ria is fine," Kanchan told her.

"And Kabir?"

"He is in Barabanki," said Kailash. "You have to go there."

"Brother, he wouldn't ever go without telling me," she replied. "Please, tell me the truth. Please!"

"Kabir couldn't be saved," Kailash finally revealed the truth.

She raised herself up from her bed and exclaimed, "Kailash! Don't tell lies, brother."

"No, *gudiya,* I am not telling lies."

She screamed loudly, "KABIR! How could you go? Come back for Ria's sake, please!" She cried uncontrollably and fell unconscious. The doctors were informed and it took her five days to recover from the shock. Ria was completely fine by that time. Her parents and siblings remained there at the hospital beside her at all times. Back home at Barabanki, Kabir was cremated and his father lit the pyre.

After a few days, Saroja and Ria were discharged from the hospital. On her request, she was taken back to her house in Bareilly. Her parents insisted on her to come back to Barabanki, but she refused. Kailash and Kanchan requested her to go with them and stay at Delhi-NCR, where they were now living, but she didn't agree to that either. She made it clear to all that she wished to continue living in Bareilly. Brijesh had also come to see her and to return some articles and their cell phones recovered from the accident site.

Brijesh cautiously advised her to go back to Barabanki too, but she just looked at him and he understood. Nothing could change her mind to leave Bareilly. Her parents and siblings had to give up eventually and finally bid goodbye to her. Kailash tried to give her some money, but she refused to take it. With tears in her eyes, Kanchan said to her, "Do call us if you need anything at all."

"Take care of yourself," Kailash told her beloved sister, while their parents simply looked on helplessly.

"Brother, I only want Kabir. Will you please bring him to me?" she replied crying. Brijesh, who had been standing next to Kailash, heard it all too. Saroja and Ria remained at Bareilly, while the others returned to their respective cities of work.

Diwali came and went uneventfully, while Saroja took charge of the furniture store and resumed her studies. On top of it all, she managed to take care of Ria as well. She hired a maid to take care of Ria in the mornings, and took her to the furniture store with her on her way back from college every afternoon. This schedule continued uninterruptedly till she successfully completed her Post Graduation in July, 2008. It was a leap year. On 29th February, Kabir's birthday, she simply cried all day and vowed to not celebrate Ria's or her own birthday that year.

Managing a furniture store was not her cup of tea, which eventually led to a loss and was consequently shut down. She started teaching English Literature at a private coaching institute to earn her livelihood, but with time, it proved to be insufficient to take care of all her household expenses. She thought of seeking help from her parents and siblings sometimes, but soon changed her mind off it. One day while reading an English newspaper, she came across a classified advertisement for the post of an English proofreader at a well-known publishing house in Delhi. She applied for the same, and as luck would have it, she got called to Delhi for an interview, and in another few days, she received an offer to join.

She called up her parents to inform them of the same. They were pleased to know about her new assignment and told her to stay at either Kanchan's or Kailash's house, whatever was more convenient for her. She didn't say anything in reply. She then called up her siblings, both of whom were very happy to know about her coming to Delhi and assured her that things would get sorted once she arrived in the city.

PART 2

Chapter I

3C Lajpat Nagar

It was pouring down heavily over the National Capital Region on Saturday, the 2nd of August, 2008, when Saroja and Ria reached Kanchan's apartment in Noida, Sector 18. Kailash was there to welcome them too. The three siblings were meeting after a long time. Kailash and Kanchan hugged Saroja and cried. It is said to be the best way to let go of your anger against a loved one, to just cry and shed the tears out. That is exactly what happened when these siblings let their tears out to shed away all their animosity and anger.

Saroja finally felt at ease and informed them of her new employment at a publishing house based in Connaught Place, and that she had to join them from Monday, the 4th of August. Kailash took Ria in his arms and started playing with her. That evening, they went to shop at Great India Place, the largest shopping mall in those times, situated in Sector 18, Noida. After the shopping, they had a quiet dinner and returned home. Kailash took the sofa in the hall, while Kanchan and Saroja sat down to talk before sleeping.

"How will I manage Ria from Monday onwards?"she asked Kanchan.

"Don't stress about it. I will ask the maid to take care of Ria full time. It's only a matter of a few days. It will all be fine soon."

That night, they discussed everything from their Varanasi to Barabanki days. Saroja just listened to everything quietly. Kabir's name did not come up, much to Saroja's peace of mind, since she felt reluctant to talk about him still. Kailash and Kanchan could sense it too. Ria was soon fast sleep, while the three siblings talked and talked till the early hours of the morning before going to bed. The next day, Sunday, passed away in laziness.

Kailash left for his house in Gurgaon late in the evening, saying, "Kanchan, do come to Gurgaon with *gudia* next week."

"Yes, brother," she replied.

He wished Saroja all the best, kissed little Ria goodbye and left. On Monday, 4th August, 2008, Kanchan dropped Saroja at her Connaught Place office at 10:30 AM sharp, while Ria remained at home in the good care of Kanchan's house maid. Kanchan went straight to Parliament Street from there to cover news for her media channel.

Saroja sat at the lounge next to the reception till she got called in to meet the CEO of the publishing house. “Have a seat, please,” the CEO, Amitav Sanyal, welcomed her into his office.

“Thanks, sir,” she replied and took a seat. After a brief discussion, he rang for the office boy and instructed him, “Call in Kabir sir.”

“Yes, sir,” the office boy replied and exited the cabin. When Saroja heard the name Kabir, her heart skipped a beat but she tried to act normally.

“May I come in, sir?” asked one gentleman while knocking at the CEO’s door.

“Oh, yes please,” the CEO replied. The man entered the room and came to stand next to Saroja’s chair. The CEO introduced her to the gentleman, saying, “This is Mr.Mustafa Kabir.”

Saroja greeted him and Kabir reciprocated the gesture.

“Saroja,” the CEO continued, “He is the Chief Editor here, and you will report to him. Kabir, just guide her around the assignments, please. She is our new proofreader.”

“Oh, yes of course, sir,” Kabir said. “Let’s go,” he gestured and turned to move out of the cabin.

Saroja followed him out, thinking, ‘Why on earth does the name Kabir keep returning to my life?’ Mustafa Kabir led her into his own cabin, explained her job profile to her, then allotted her a work station after completion of the routine H.R. formalities with the H.R. department.

Mustafa Kabir was born on 31st May, 1982, in Allahabad, Uttar Pradesh. His family had moved to Delhi in 1995 and was settled in Lajpat Nagar. He had grown up as a student of Delhi Public School and had later completed his Masters in English Literature from Delhi University before joining the publishing house run by Amitav Sanyal. His experiences in life had turned him into a determined secularist. Mustafa Kabir lived a bachelor's life with his parents in Lajpat Nagar.

Saroja began the first day of her work by proofreading an upcoming fiction novel, and she was really impressive at it. Kabir applauded her work and conveyed the same to their CEO, Amitav Sanyal. "You have found a gem, sir," he said to the CEO that evening over a cup of tea with him. He simply reverted with a mischievous smile. Saroja had already left after being done for the day by then.

On reaching Kanchan's place in Noida, she picked her daughter up in her arms and kissed her all over her cheeks. Kanchan had not returned home yet. She entered the kitchen and started the preparation for dinner. Later that evening, Kanchan came back home and they had a quiet meal together. Kailash called Saroja on her cell phone to ask about her day and how it had gone. She informed him that it was a good day to start with, which soon became a routine for her. She found some solace in Delhi in the company of her siblings, and also established a frequent communication with her parents. This was something that she had missed over all those years.

It became a routine for the three siblings to meet every Sunday, either at Kanchan's house in Noida or at Kailash's house in Gurgaon. Little Ria gradually started to recognize Kanchan and Kailash too. One such Sunday evening, on 12th October, Kailash informed them that he had been offered a plump post at another MNC based out of Singapore, so he might have to move out of the country by the year's end. He called up Mr. and Mrs. Mishra at Barabanki to inform them of his plans to move to Singapore soon.

The concerned parents insisted that he settles down before moving out to another country, as they had lately been receiving some good proposals for him too. One in particular, recommended to them by Mr. and Mrs. Singh, was from a family settled in Delhi. The prospective bride's father, Mr. Govind Shukla, was a retired *Patwari* from Kapashera, while her mother, Neelam Shukla, was the Principal at a Public School in Dwarka. The bride-to-be, Ms. Payal, was a well-qualified MBA from MDI, Gurgaon, and was placed with an MNC Bank as their Business Development Executive.

Kailash insisted that he wasn't ready for marriage yet. Mr. and Mrs. Mishra then spoke about the issue of Kailash's marriage with Kanchan and Saroja, who also thought that it was high time that Kailash should get married, more so because the proposal had come through the Singh family who had always stood by them through their thick and thin. It was thus obligatory for them to at least give this a thought.

After much persuasion by his sisters, Kailash finally consented to at least meeting the girl along with them. Kanchan immediately informed her parents at Barabanki of her brother's decision, and a schedule was fixed through the Singh family for a meeting. It was decided that they would meet the next Sunday, 19th October, at the residence of the bride's relatives, Mr. and Mrs. Pandey, in Lajpat Nagar Central Market near the 3C shopping mall. Mr. and Mrs.Pandey were financially quite sound and owned a chain of medical stores, with more than ten of them within the South Delhi area.

Back at office, Saroja was meticulous with her work and gradually won over the confidence of her boss Mr.Mustafa Kabira, also receiving many accolades from their CEO Amitav Sanyal as well.

On 19th October, the next Sunday, at 6.30 PM, Kailash and his sisters–Kanchan and Saroja, along with little Ria, reached Mr. and Mrs. Pandey's house. They parked their Innova in the parking lot and entered the house where the Shuklas had already arrived with their beloved daughter, Ms. Payal Shukla. Kailash had worn simple blue denims along with a white shirt and a blue blazer, while

Kanchan was dressed in a blue *sari* which she had matched with a blue *bindi* and blue bangles. She looked very pretty with her straight long hair which covered most of her back.

Saroja, who was carrying Ria with her, was dressed in a pink sari with a white bindi and pink bangles. She had pulled her long hair to one side and had let them lose over her shoulder to fall over her pink blouse. She looked so beautiful that the entire Shukla and Pandey clan was mesmerized by her presence. The Mishra siblings were greeted by the Shuklas and the Pandeys before being put at ease in the visitors' room. A house maid brought in juice and tea with some snacks to serve to the guests.

Everyone from the bride's side had occupied one sofa, while the visitors sat in front of them on another sofa. In the middle was a table holding a centre piece. The maid served each one of them with the refreshments and the customary talks began over cups of tea and the crunch of snacks. In some time, the bride-to-be,Ms. Payal Shukla, was called in. She walked into the visitor's room along with a young girl and a boy. The girl was Ankita Pandey, daughter of Mr. and Mrs. Pandey, and the boy was Arjit Pandey, their son.

Payal was dressed in a purple *salwar kameez* and looked sober and attractive. Mr. and Mrs. Shukla introduce her to Kailash and his sisters, and as it happens when a boy meets a girl for a marriage proposal, they mostly kept quite while the family discussed pretty much everything on earth, their likes, dislikes, backgrounds, etc. After some time then, both Payal and Kailash were given the opportunity to talk in private, so they went inside a room, while the conversation in the visitors' room continued. Ankita and Arjit took the lead to talk further. Arjit was particularly excited in making conversation, specially whenever it was directed at Saroja, but Saroja wasn't too interested.

"Are you married?" he asked.

"Yes, and she is my daughter," she replied, pointing to Ria.

Mr.Pandey then asked Saroja, "What does your husband do?"

"His name was Kabir Prajapati, and he is no more," she replied.

"Hmm, you married a Prajapati?" he continued.

Saroja simply looked at him without a reaction. "It was a love marriage," Kanchan replied instead.

Ankita and Arjit fell quiet, whereas Mr. and Mrs. Shukla exchanged glances with Mr. and Mrs. Pandey, as if wanting to say something, but kept quiet.

In another ten minutes, Kailash and Payal walked out with a smile on their faces. It was almost dinner time by then. The Shuklas insisted on the guests to stay for dinner, but Kailash politely declined and they soon took their leave from the Pandeys' residence. Saroja thanked them for their hospitality and kind gesture. Kailash took out their Innova from the parking lot and they all left for Noida, to Kanchan's house. Kailash wanted to stay at Kanchan's house that night for some reason that nobody knew.

On their way to Noida, Saroja asked Kailash, "What happened, brother?"

"Nothing, *gudiya*."

"Tell us naa, brother. Bolo," Kanchan insisted.

"Payal does not want to marry me, though I must say, I liked her," Kailash replied.

"Why does she not want to marry you?" asked Saroja.

"She is in a relationship with her colleague from MDI," he said. "What's his name? I forgot. She had told me," he continued. "Yeah, his name is Jamshed Irani, and her parents aren't agreeing for the match. And they are right too, aren't they? To marry a Hindu from another caste is one thing, but to marry out of the religion, no way. It's not done," he went on saying, not realizing that they have reached Noida. They had a quiet dinner at home before going to sleep.

The next day at office, Mustafa Kabir met Saroja in the CEO's cabin and asked her, "Did you come to Lajpat 3C last evening?"

Saroja gave him a strange look. “How do you know?” she questioned.

“Ohh, relax. I stay behind the Post Office near 3C Lajpat, and I know the Pandeys very well,” he replied. “I saw you from the window of my house while you were entering the Pandeys’ house with some friends. You were also carrying a baby girl.”

“They are my siblings, Kailash and Kanchan, and the baby is my daughter Ria,” Saroja replied.

“Oh, I see. Anyway, I thought I’d just share this with you. In fact, I would have loved to host you and your siblings at my house too. Do come by my place as well when you drop in to see the Pandeys again.”

Saroja didn’t answer to that. Instead, she simply collected some files from the CEO Amitav Sanyal’s desk and left his cabin.

“Mustafa dear, I guess you have developed some feelings for Saroja,” Amitav asked Mustafa who was still standing in his cabin.

“Nooo way, man! I just adore her work, that’s it,” he gave an instant reply.

Amitav Sanyal smiled and asked,“By the way, what is this 3C?”

It’s a theatre with a roof-top restaurant and a shopping mall,” said Mustafa and turned to leave the cabin.

“Oh, it must be very romantic,” Amitav teased.

“Bye,” said Mustafa and left.

At the dinner table that evening, Kanchan asked Saroja what she thought of Arijit Pandey, whom they had met at the Pandeys’ house the previous evening.

“I don’t know. Why are you asking me this?” she replied.

“No, I guess we can just talk about him,” Kanchan said with a mischievous smile.

“But why?” she asked again, but irritated. “Look, Kanchan, I don’t think we should talk about Arjit.”

“*Gudia*, I really liked him. I feel we may need to meet the Pandeys again,” Kanchan replied.

“Hmmm, it’s fine then. I will convey the same to *bhaiya* to fix a meeting.”

Saroja called up Kailash and conveyed Kanchan’s wish to him. Kailash spoke about it to his parents in Barabanki who were able to get the contact number of Mr. and Mrs. Pandey through Ramesh Singh’s help. Kailash also informed his parents about Payal’s view and requested them to respect her decision. Kailash persuaded the Pandeys for a meeting, for her younger sister’s proposal this time.

On the eve of Diwali, the 28th of October, Kailash, Kanchan, Saroja and Ria went to Lajpat Nagar 3C again. Kanchan escaped the meeting herself and went to the roof-top restaurant at 3C Mall instead. Kailash parked the Innova in the parking lot of the Pandeys' residence and they were greeted by the couple and their daughter, Ankita. While they took their seats in the visitors' room, Ankita rushed out to another room. The house maid entered with some juice and snacks. Without wasting time, Kailash informed them about Payal's decision from the last meeting.

"We know, beta," said Mr.Pandey.

Kailash then opened up with Kanchan's proposal for his son, Arjit. Mr. and Mrs. Pandey heard him patiently and rather liked the idea of Kanchan marrying Arjit. Kailash spoke very highly of Kanchan. She was indeed a very nice girl, equally focused on her carrier and concerned about her family.

"Dear, we had initially thought of Saroja for Arijit, but she..." they started while pointing at Saroja. "But she has already gotten married outside of our caste and is with a child too."

Saroja didn't react.

"Uncle, it was her fate. We should talk about Kanchan and Arjit instead," he said.

Mr. and Mrs. Pandey sat thinking for a few minutes, when Ankita came in with the house maid to serve them tea. After the tea, Mr.Pandey asked Kailash, "Dear son, what do you think of Ankita, my daughter?"

"She is nice," Kailash replied.

"She is an interior designer and has done her graduation in interior designing from NID Ahmadabad. Right now, she is working for a reputed real estate chain in Gurgaon. My son, Arjit, is a pharmacist and handles the chain of medical stores that were established and are run by our family."

Kailash understood what Mr. and Mrs.Pandey wanted to say. "Uncle, if you think that Kanchan is right for Arjit, I guess that your idea can be thought of too! It sounds good, doesn't it, Saroja?" he asked her abruptly.

"If you think it appropriate, brother, it is fine," she replied.

The Pandeys agreed to Kanchan's proposal. Kailash convinced his parents about Ankita too. That's how the Mishras from Barabanki and the Pandeys from Delhi became relatives through this reciprocal proposal.

On 11th December, 2008, a grand wedding was held at a farmhouse owned by the Pandeys on the NH8 highway near Mahipalpur. The Singh family, along with Brijesh, graced the occasion too. Saroja did not invite any of her office colleagues, but the Pandeys had invited Mustafa Kabir, since he was their neighbor at 3C. At the wedding, he spent most of his time standing alone in one corner and looking at Saroja. The Pandeys introduced Mustafa to the

Mishra and Singh families, including Saroja as well.

"I know him, he is my boss," she said, looking directly at Mustafa Kabir.

"Oh, we didn't know," the Pandeys replied.

Mustafa just smiled. "Why didn't you invite any of us from the office?" he asked Saroja.

"We are just professional colleagues, Mr.Mustafa," she replied.

"You can call me Mr.Kabir."

"I knew only one Kabir, my deceased husband."

"Cute daughter," he changed the topic, looking at Ria.

"My daughter," she said.

"God bless you all," said Mustafa.

Chapter 2

Cold Coffee

Soon after the wedding was over, most of the family members and relatives returned to their hometowns. Kailash and Kanchan, with their respective spouses, left for their honeymoon to Malaysia and Shri Lanka respectively. Kailash was to leave for Singapore immediately after his honeymoon and had prepared for the same. His *gudia* was all alone once again. The Mishras had gone back to Barabanki with Mr. and Mrs. Singh.

Brijesh, however, had stayed back in Delhi and had taken residence at the UP Bhavan.On Christmas Eve, he called up Saroja on her cellphone, the contact of which he had taken from her at the wedding. “Can we meet for coffee today?” he asked her.

“Okay,” she answered. “Which place and what time?” she continued on the other side of the phone.

“At 7 PM, at the CCD near Satyam Cinemas in Nehru Place. Don’t worry, I will drop you back to

Noida later," Brijesh assured her. Saroja knew why Brijesh wanted to meet her.

That evening at 7PM sharp, Saroja reached the CCD in Nehru place. She had worn a white *salwar kameez* with a blue *dupatta*. She found Brijesh, in blue denims and a white shirt, already there waiting for her. As she entered the cafe, he got up to receive her and offered her a seat before taking his own.

"Make yourself comfortable," he told her. "What will you have?" he asked further.

"Nothing," she replied.

"Not fair. Have something," he insisted.

"Alright, one cold coffee," she said.

Brijesh called for the waiter and said, "Two cold coffees, please."

"Sir, please place your order at the counter," the waiter replied.

"Oh!" Brijesh exclaimed and got up to go to the counter. He ordered two cold coffees, paid the bill and came back to their table.

"So, what is happening?" he asked Saroja.

"Everything is fine," she answered.

"How is Ria?" he asked further.

"She is fine too," she answered again.

There was absolute silence between them for a few minutes.

"Sir, your cold coffee," said the waiter, placing two tall glasses of cold coffee on their table.

"Thanks," Brijesh said, looking at the waiter.

Saroja took little sips of her coffee, while Brijesh left his untouched.

He asked again, "You must be feeling alone now."

Saroja looked into his eyes and replied defiantly, "No. Ria is there with me."

Brijesh smiled, "I mean, have you thought for getting married again?"

Saroja had by now finished half her glass of cold coffee. Looking straight at him again, she said, "Brijesh, let's finish the coffee quickly. I am getting late. It's 8 PM already. Ria is alone at home with the maid."

Brijesh had only taken a few sips of his coffee by the time Saroja drained her glass empty. "Let's go, I will drop you home," he said.

"No, I can go on my own," she replied.

Brijesh insisted strongly that he should drop her, to which she finally agreed. Brijesh called his driver and they headed towards Noida, to Kanchan apartment which Saroja was occupying for the time being since Kanchan's wedding. Saroja got down near her house. Brijesh got down after her and smiled.

"I shall wait for you all my life. Think again," he said.

"Goodnight," she replied. "No one is at home right now, else I would have invited you in. Please don't mind it," she said further.

"No worries. I can understand," Brijesh replied.

Brijesh kept waiting by the car until she disappeared beyond the gates of her society. He then got back inside his car, sanctioned to him by his office, and instructed the driver to head to Budaun.

"Yes sir," replied the driver. They left Noida for Budaun the same night.

Chapter 3

For Ria's Sake

On February 14th, 2009, Saroja was at her office. It was Valentine's Day as well as a Saturday, so most of the office staff was in a mood to celebrate. It was customary for them to celebrate the day every year. In fact, every festival was celebrated by them with equal zeal and enthusiasm. The entire office was decorated with red heart-shaped balloons to create an atmosphere of love and romance. The balloons, along with a red rose, were placed on each work station and at every cabin. All the birthdays of staff members as well as festivals were celebrated at office with a customary cake-cutting.

A huge heart-shape cake had been ordered for this day. All the staff members assembled in the conference room for the cake-cutting. Amitav and Mustafa entered last. The tradition had been to assigned the task of cutting the cake to the newest member in the office. As it happened, Saroja was the only choice.

"Saroja, let's cut the cake," Amitav said, explaining to her the office tradition.

Saroja came forward and stood between Amitav and Mustafa. The entire office clapped and cheered 'Happy Valentine's Day' as she cut the cake. Amitav took a small piece of the cake and offered it to Saroja. She accepted it gratefully.

"Give some to us as well now," said Amitav and laughed.

She cut two small pieces from the cake and offered one each to Amitav and Mustafa.

"You know, I am diabetic, but I will take it since it's you who is offering it," said Amitav, looking at Saroja. He then shifted his gaze to Mustafa who was standing right next to her. He was smiling. Both Amitav and Mustafa ate the cake that they were offered by her.

After the ceremony, Amitav called Saroja to his cabin. "Please be seated," Amitav said as soon as she entered. She took the middle seat across the table from Amitav. Amitav was pretending to do something on his laptop placed on the table, but in reality, he was doing nothing.

"Will you have tea or coffee?" he asked her.

"Coffee will do."

He rang for the office boy and instructed him, "Two coffees, please," when he entered. Within the next five minutes, he returned to the cabin with two cups of coffee, served them on the table and left. Saroja sipped quietly on her coffee, waiting for Amitav to speak. He seemed to be deep in thought, stirring his coffee with a spoon.

"Saroja, I want to spend the rest of my life with you," he finally said, albeit hurriedly.

She looked up in surprise to meet Amitav's gaze. She put down her cup, not knowing what to say in reply.

He started again, "I am a brahmin from Calcutta. I was born in Siliguri on 7th July, 1981. My parents are lawyers and are settled back in Calcutta. I stay alone in Hauz Khas and have been there since I first came to Delhi after my post-graduation from Calcutta University in the year 2003. I bought the same house where I used to stay on rent." He went on to tell her all about how he started his career as a proofreader, just like her, with a tabloid publication house there in Connaught Place itself, then went on to become an independent publisher himself, as he was more interested in telling stories to the world. Saroja listened to him patiently, while thinking if she was really ready for another relationship yet.

"Sir, you do know that I am a widow with a little daughter," she said unassumingly.

"Yes, I know and I have no issues with that. I will adopt her as my own," he said. "There is no hurry, Saroja. Take your time to think over it and let me know when you have an answer. And listen, whatever be your decision, I will respect it and you shall always be a part of my team, rest assured."

Saroja got up and said, "I will leave early today, if you don't mind."

"Alright, you may go," he said.

As soon as she left the cabin and came back to her work station, she collected her things, picked up her bag and left the office, not in anger, but in confusion. She didn't know why she had asked to leave early from the office, when she didn't have any other plans for the day. Perhaps it had escaped her mouth in that moment.

She headed straight to Kanchan's house in Lajpat Nagar from her office and told her everything. Kanchan advised her to accept the offer. "Mom, dad and *bhai* will agree to it too since Amitav is also a brahmin. It won't be too difficult for them to accept," she said. "Nowadays, who is willing to marry a widow anyway, and is ready to adopt her daughter as well? Think practically," she advised. Kanchan's husband and in-laws suggested that she thinks over it too. Kanchan informed her parents at Barabanki about this as well, who also thought it to be good for Saroja.

Later that evening, Saroja left Lajpat Nagar for Noida. She only thought of Amitav's proposal throughout her way. She wanted to be cautious in her approach. 'Kabir wasn't brahmin, maybe that's why mom and dad didn't accept him. But they may this time, since Amitav is a brahmin,' she wondered. She reached home to find Ria waiting for her.

"Make me a cup of tea," she asked the maid.

"Yes, *didi*."

"Umm, actually do one thing, make coffee for me," she instructed again.

"Yes, *didi*."

She kept thinking of Amitav's proposal, wondering whether she actually had any feeling for Amitav at all. He had only been a decent boss to her until that afternoon, but things had changed drastically since his proposal. 'Ria will be turning two the coming May. She needs a better life and better education. Will I alone be able to do justice to it all?' she asked herself.

"*Didi*, should I serve the dinner now?"the maid asked.

"Hmm, yes," she replied absentmindedly. She had a quiet dinner with Ria and went to bed, but could not sleep properly. She kept thinking through the night, but couldn't come to a conclusion. Sleep eventually came, but in the early hours of the next morning. She spent the Sunday with her beloved daughter and kept thinking about her future.

Saroja could not arrive at any solution even after the next few weeks were past. Amitav kept asking her for an answer repeatedly, but she was unable to either accept or refuse his proposal.

On 11th March, 2009, the day of Holi, she got a call on her cellphone early in the morning. It was Amitav.

"Happy Holi, Saroja," he wished her.

"Wish you the same," she reciprocated.

He asked if she would like to spend the day at his residence in Hauz Khas. She declined the offer, saying that it wasn't possible for her to travel all the way to Hauz Khas, with everyone playing colors on the streets.

"I am sending a car to pick you up. Please come with Ria," he insisted.

While talking to him, she received another call with Kanchan's name flashing on the screen.

"I will call you back," she told Amitav and disconnect the call.

Kanchan called again, which Saroja answered this time.

"Happy Holi, *gudia*, to you and Ria," she wished and continued. "I have been calling you for a while, but your phone was engaged throughout. Were you talking to someone?"

Saroja wished Kanchan and her in-laws a happy Holi, then informed her about Amitav's call.

Kanchan advised her to go, if conveniently possible, and resolve all her confusions once and for all.

Once she was done talking to Kanchan, she called up her parents in Barabanki to wish them Holi and sought their permission to go to Amitav's place for the day. After wishing her and Ria, Mr. Mishra said from the other side, "Dear, please inform Kanchan and Kailash about it. We don't have any problem."

"I have already spoken to Kanchan. It won't be possible to talk to Kailash right now since he is in Singapore," she answered.

"Okay then, go ahead," her father approved.

Relived, she thanked her parents and called Amitav back to ask him to send his car over to pick her up. She got herself and Ria ready, called her maid on her cellphone and told her not to come, since she would be out for the day.

By 11 AM, when most people were out on the streets playing with colors, Saroja and Ria reached Amitav's house. She spent the entire day with him. Amitav played with Ria throughout the day. This was the first time that she was having lunch with Amitav. He had cooked it for her himself. Curry, rice, salad, ladyfinger and soft phoolkas, everything cooked by him was delicious.

"You see, I asked my driver to go pick you up because I had to prepare this food for you. I have asked him to go home and enjoy Holi with his family now. He stays nearby in Sarojini Nagar," Amitav went on talking, while Saroja simply sat on the sofa. Later on, they ate together, shared jokes, their likes and dislikes, their past and present, their future plans and every other thing on earth.

Later that evening, he dropped her back to her place in Noida. When she was getting down with Ria, he handed a box of chocolates to Ria. Saroja looked at him as he drew closer to her, looked deep into her eyes and said, "For Ria's sake, will you marry me?"

"I will let you know. Please give me a day's time," she replied and left with a quiet *goodnight*.

"Goodnight," he replied and drove back to Hauz Khas.

That night, she was chatting with her brother Kailash on a chat messenger. After wishing him and Ankita *bhabi* a happy Holi, she sought his views on Amitav's proposal too. Kailash reverted positively, saying that Kanchan had already shared with him the details of the matter while chatting with him just a while ago.

She was convinced and somehow relieved that she now had everyone's permission, unlike her previous runaway marriage with Kabir, where she hadn't asked any of her family members.

She thought of calling Brijesh to share with him the news about Amitav, but soon changed her mind.

She fed Ria, had her own dinner, and went to bed. Before going to sleep, she picked up her cellphone, searched for Amitav's number in her phonebook, and texted him, 'Yes, I will marry you,' then switched off the cell. After months perhaps, she had a good night's sleep on that Holi night.

When Amitav received the text massage, he checked it and smiled.

Chapter 4

Wedding in Bengali Style

Amitav summoned the entire office staff in the conference room the next morning at work. When everybody, including Mustafa, had assembled, he requested them all to be seated.

"Is there some important discussion to be had today?" asked Mustafa.

"Yes," Amitav replied, then continued after a pause, "Friends, the reason I have called you all here is that I want to share an important moment of my life with you all."He looked at Saroja who was sitting across the table from him and asked her, "May I, with your permission?"

She nodded shyly and said, "Yes."

Mustafa Kabir didn't know what was happening and looked on confusedly.

“Saroja and I are getting married,” Amitav declared.

“Wow! Hurray! Congrats!” the entire conference room burst into cheers and claps. All, except Mustafa. He felt uneasy, which did not escape the notice of both Amitav and Saroja.

“Sir, we want a party,” demanded one of the staff.

“When is the D-date?” asked another.

“The day after tomorrow, 14th March, at Mandir Marg Kalibari Temple at 5.30 AM in the morning,” replied Amitav.

“Is it on a very short notice, sir?” asked one of the staff.

“Yes, it is. It was only yesterday that Saroja and I decided to have a simple wedding. Only our close family members will be there for the actual ceremony, but we’ll have a reception for everybody else on the 27th of March at Sainik Farms, so keep yourself free that evening.”

Saroja had already informed her siblings and parents about the wedding plans. In such a rushed and hush–hush preparation, Amitav had only called his parents from his side.

In the wee hours of the 14th of March, Amitav and Saroja tied the nuptial knots in the presence of their close family and friends. It was a simple Bengali style wedding. Mr. and Mrs. Sanyal, the Mishras, the Singhs, the Pandeys, along with Kailash with Ankita who had flown in all the way from Singapore, graced the occasion of the wedding ceremony. The reception on 27th March was attended by all their family members, friends and colleagues. The only people who were missing were Mr. Mustafa and Mr. Brijesh, who had not turned up despite personal invitations.

In just a month's time, everything had changed in Saroja's life. She became Saroja Sanyal. Ria got a step–father and moved into her new house in Hauz Khas with her mother. It was all like a dream. The Sanyals were happy to welcome their daughter-in-law, while the Mishras were happy to welcome their son-in-law. This time, everything had happened with the blessings of the two families.

Chapter 5

December, 2012

Three and a half years passed peacefully after Saroja and Amitav got married. Ria turned five that year and entered class I at DPS Hauz Khas. The city of Delhi, however, witnessed many issues over this time, involving agitations, gheraos, and various mass movements against corruption at the Ramleela Maidan. The government of the day had taken a back foot while dealing with all the corruption charges, while every citizen wanted to be crusader or an activist to raise a voice against corruption. Against such a backdrop emerged a new India, reminding one of the days when Jaiprakash Narayan had started the *Sampurn Kranti* movement – total revolution.

Kanchan, now a freelance columnist, and Arjit had now become parents of a two year old son, while Kailash was also leading a happy married life in Singapore with Ankita and a son as well. In Barabanki, the Mishras and the Singhs remained in their own comfort zone, happy with the school's responsibility, which had now started its own Degree collage too. Mr.Mishra had been made the Principal of the Degree college, while Mr.Singh had been elevated to take the position of the school Principal. Brijesh Singh, now posted at Bulandshehar, remained single still, his love for Saroja unfazed and unchanged. He hadn't come to attend her wedding because his feelings for his beloved childhood love never changed. With time, Saroja also came to respect his feelings and continued to maintain a healthy friendship and communication with him. Whenever Brijesh got the opportunity to connect with Saroja, he spoke to her over the phone, through texts or chat messages online. In fact, he often advised her to attempt the UPSC exams too.

Perhaps Saroja finally took it seriously and started preparing for the UPSC exams that year. She would often take Brijesh's advice with regard to the preparation, and remained in contact with him through this educational pursuit. The result was that she successfully attempted the preliminary exams and got to sit for the main examinations as well.

Saroja and Amitav had not had a child together even after more than three years of marriage. She took charge of the editorial department at the publishing house, since Mustafa Kabir had resigned immediately after her marriage with Amitav, and had left for an unknown destination. In fact, he had even sold off his house at Lajpat Nagar 3C, and had moved out of Delhi with his parents. Saroja and Amitav had put in their heart, mind and soul to achieve success for their publishing house. In the last three years, the couple had attended all the literary events across India together. Saroja stood by Amitav in this publication venture through his thick and thin, but all this unknowingly took a toll on her personal life.

Her mother-in-law called ever so often from Calcutta to know when she was going to give them the good news. Amitav's parents had held on to their expectation of becoming grandparents in all these years. Saroja was under the pressure to oblige to their demands, but she didn't get pregnant, despite Amitav's various attempts.

"Why don't you consult a doctor, Amitav?" she would often request him, but he wouldn't listen to her.

"You think I have a medical problem?" he would interrupt, though he knew deep down that the problem had to be with him, since Saroja had nothing to prove for her motherhood. It was rather he who had failed to get her pregnant. The pressures of fathering a child misguided Amitav to the wrong path and he took to drinking. Despite having been a teetotaller all his life, he started depending on alcohol to deal with the mounting pressure of fathering a child. Helpless herself, Saroja could not do anything about it. She never discussed her personal problems with anyone, and continued to portray to the outside world that everything was fine between Amitav and herself. Minor scuffles would often take place between them, but they would soon cool down, for there was no love lost between them yet.

"Saroja, let's be done with the packing, yaar. We need to leave for Goa tomorrow itself. The Literary Festival won't wait for us to begin," Amitav called out to her. The Goa Literary Festival was to due to commence on 13th December, 2012.

"Yes, I am already done with the packing. You needn't worry. What time is our flight tomorrow?" she asked.

"It's a 9 AM flight," he replied. "Let's move now. We are quite late already. It's almost 11 AM and we need to wind up a lot of things at office before we depart tomorrow," Amitav told Saroja as they headed to their Connaught Place office in the morning of 12th December.

From writers and editors, to books enthusiasts and intellectuals, the who's who of the Publishing industry had come to grace the Goa Literary Festival which was to last from 13th December to 17th December, 2012. At the Dabolim Airport baggage conveyor belt, Amitav spotted Mustafa Kabir waiting for his baggage to arrive. Waving his hand, he called out, "Hi, Mustafa."

Mustafa turned around to see Amitav walking in his direction, closely followed by Saroja behind. “Hello! How are you doing, Amitav?” he asked as his old boss reached him.

“I am fine. How are you doing?” Amitav asked in return.

“I am good,” Mustafa replied with a smile as he saw Saroja reaching up to them.

“Hi, how are you doing, Mustafa?” asked Saroja.

“I am good and I hope you are doing well too,” he replied.

“What brings you to Goa?” Amitav interrupted.

“The Literary Festival,” he replied nonchalantly.

“But we didn’t see you at any of the literary festivals in the last three years since you left us.”

“Yes, in fact, the circumstances were such in the last three years that I couldn’t attend any festivals at all. This year, however, I decided to attend this one.”

“Alright. By the way, where are you nowadays? No call, no contact otherwise, you seem to have disappeared, man,” Amitav asked further, while Mustafa continued to look at Saroja.

“I am in Lucknow, working for an E-portal as an Editor. In fact, I have shifted there with my parents,” he replied.

"You still single?"Amitav enquired.

"Yes," he answered. "I am staying at a rented bungalow here at Dona Paula," he continued.

"Great, we've put up at the State Guest House," replied Amitav.

"Oh, you can join me if you wish," Mustafa requested Amitav.

"What do you think, Saroja?"Amitav asked her.

"I guess, let's first reach the guest house, then in a day or two perhaps we may join Mustafa over dinner," she replied.

"Sounds great. Let's meet for old time's sake," Amitav said. Mustafa was still waiting for his baggage to arrive, while Amitav and Saroja's baggage had come in the meantime. "Okay, buddy. Catch you at the venue at the International Centre," said Amitav while picking up their bags.

"Yes, for sure," Mustafa replied with a smile and kept looking at Saroja till she exited the airport gate. His baggage soon arrived, which he picked up and left straight for his rented out bungalow and then headed to the venue for the festival.

A keynote address on the first day by the eminent writer Mridula Garg inspired the many who had come to attend the festival. Very rightly, she said:

"What is Literature? It is the soul or the unconscious mind entering into another body

or consciousness. It means more than being in someone else's shoes. It implies becoming the other. Literature requires that we write the self as if it was the other, and the other as if it was the self. And the other is not necessarily outside us. Many live within us. Sometimes, in a blink of an eye, we discover that the someone we thought lay at the extreme end of the margin is actually the closest to us; in fact, is our alter ego. That is the point when we begin to create literature or art.

This year, the Goa Festival is focused on Kashmir. When a writer creates non-conformist characters, their actions force him to change too. Otherwise, he may write subversion but still conform to all the social norms and aspirations, like the rest of the middle roaders in real life. Sometimes, after he has written of a particularly daring behavior, he is forced to reflect, 'Okay, if my character could make that choice, why can't I?' When we look at it this way, we realize that it's not only the people belonging to different cultures, who are the outsiders. Each one of us is an outsider. Probing different personas within us can take us on a journey of re-discovery of the self as the other and the other as the self."

After the initial inaugural events, the festival took off, giving opportunities to the various attendees to express their ideas and debate on the issues of the day. As the day progressed and tea time commenced, a young and enthusiastic author from Chandigarh approached Amitav, who was at that time having a conversation with Mustafa, Saroja and some other authors.

"Sir, I am Zubin Saxena," he introduced himself hesitantly. "I am a writer and I have a script ready for publishing. Would you be interested in having a look at it?"

"Friend, I'm afraid I won't be able to help you with that right now. Meet me at my office in Delhi sometime in January perhaps," said Amitav and handed him his visiting card. Mustafa Kabir looked at both of them, while Saroja remained standing there quietly.

"Zubin Saxena, that is an interesting name," commented Mustafa.

"Yeah, I am part Kayastha and part Parsi. My mom is Parsi and dad is Kayastha," he replied while looking at Saroja. Their eyes met for a brief moment.

"Hmm, alright. May I have a look at your script?" Mustafa asked. Zubin handed him a copy of it. "Thanks, I will surely go through this and get back to you. This is my business card," replied Mustafa.

Amitav, we can surely have a look at his script too. He is requesting us with such hope in his eyes! Let's at least have a look at it," said Saroja. He nodded in agreement. Saroja took a copy of the script from Zubin.

"Thank you, madam," he replied. Saroja smiled in response.

"What's your good name, madam?" Zubin asked, while Amitav and Mustafa were busy having a conversation between themselves.

"I am Saroja Sanyal, wife of Amitav Sanyal," she replied, gesturing at her husband, and smiled back.

Ria came running towards them from where she was playing in a corner and asked Saroja, "Mamma, I want to go to the washroom."

Zubin looked at Ria for a moment, then diverted his attention and said, "My contact number and email ID is mentioned on the script. If you feel that it is worth publishing, do contact me." Saying this, he left.

As he moved forward, he stopped and turned back as if to say something, but Saroja had by then moved towards the washroom with Ria.

Amitav and Mustafa decided to have dinner together the same night and informed Saroja of this when she returned from the washroom with Ria. Saroja noticed from the corner of her eye that Zubin had constantly been looking at her. She could not take her eyes off him either. She felt her heartbeat quicken whenever their eyes met. Trying to avoid further eye contact, she pretended to play with Ria.

Back at the guest house after the events of day one had gotten over, Saroja began reading Zubin's script while having tea. As she went on reading, the story mesmerised her more and more. It was a beautifully narrated romantic tragedy set against the backdrop of Kashmir militancy.

“Amitav, I feel this is a fantastic story to publish,” she said.

“Oh, really? You think so,” he replied.

“Yes, I do,” she answered.

“Alright, we’ll discuss this with Mustafa over dinner as well. He has a copy of the script too,” Amitav said.

Mustafa had organized a thoughtful dinner for Amitav and Saroja. Mustafa knew that Bengali brahmin ate fish, so he had ordered an authentic Goan fish curry for Amitav, along with red rice, mixed vegetables, mutton curry, and rotis. The couple, along with Ria, reached Mustafa’s place by 8 PM. Amitav had a taste of the fish curry, Mustafa enjoyed his mutton curry, while Saroja and Ria shared the red rice and mixed veg.

“I thought you have arranged for drinks as well,” said Amitav.

“Oh, really? I didn’t know you started drinking. I always took you for a teetotaller,” replied Mustafa, while Saroja looked on.

“I drink occasionally. Anyway, let’s meet for drinks in the evening on 17th at our guest house,” Amitav said.

"Well, I don't drink, but will surely give you company," Mustafa replied.

"After dinner, they talked on many subjects till midnight, while Ria continued to play with Saroja.

"Why don't you get married, Mustafa?"Amitav asked.

"I haven't found the right girl to marry yet," he replied and looked at Saroja.

"You deserve the best one," Saroja said.

"Hmm…let's not talk about it," he requested. "Are you two into family planning, or what? No kids yet? It has been more than three years since the wedding," Mustafa asked both of them.

"With God's grace, we will surely have a kid in the coming years," Saroja answered hurriedly.

"Have you read that script that Zubin gave?" Amitav asked. "Saroja found it quite compelling," he said further.

"It's bullshit. What crap, a romantic tragedy against the backdrop of Kashmir militancy. I wouldn't recommend it," Mustafa replied.

"You are either too harsh or you don't know anything of love and romance," said Saroja.

Mustafa smiled, but kept quiet.

"It has gotten too late, I guess we should leave now," she said further.

"Yeah, it's too late," replied Mustafa.

Amitav and Saroja thanked Mustafa for having hosted the dinner for them and wished him goodnight before leaving with Ria.

"Goodnight and God bless you all," said Mustafa and went in to sleep after they left.

On their return to the guest house, Amitav was in a confrontational mood with Saroja. "Are you sure we will have a kid by next year?" he asked Saroja while she was putting Ria to sleep.

"Amitav, if you don't bring in your male ego, we can go seek an expert's opinion on it or maybe opt for IVF or a test tube baby. There are so many solutions to this problem. Don't complicate it just for the sake of your ego. Medical science has advanced so much and you know it."

He didn't reply to it. They switched off the lights, as Ria was fast sleep in another room, and went to bed after some time.

While they were lying in their bed, he asked, "Let's try naturally one more time." Saroja came closer to him. He pulled her up close to kiss her, and they made love that night.

On 16th December, the entire nation was shocked to hear of the Nirbhaya gang rape tragedy in Delhi. News channels ran stories about the issue all day and it became a topic of debate across all platforms. The next morning, the entire print media and all the public forums had this one subject to discuss and debate on -the tragic incident of Nirbhaya's gang rape -and the closing ceremony of the Literary Festival was no exception. 'Justice for Nirbhaya' became a crusade, candle light marches were organized, and the intellectuals expressed their grief over Twitter. Activist, celebrities, and politicians gave their own TV bites on how disturbed they were with the news of the incident and how concerned they were about women's safety in the country. International Media declared our nation unsafe for women and warned the travellers from travelling to India.

Mustafa reached the guest house on 17th, where Amitav was ready to host him. Saroja and Ria were busy playing with a teddy bear then. Amitav was sitting on a sofa placed in the hall of the guest house, and Mustafa went to occupy a seat beside him. Amitav offered him a drink which he politely declined. Amitav insisted, but was unsuccessful. Amitav had a few pegs of a mist, while insisting Mustafa to have some cola. He did not know that Amitav had already spiked all the cola with wine. Mustafa drank a few glasses of cola, leaving a little to have later.

While both the men were busy with their respective drinks, Saroja and Ria had dinner together. Ria was then put to bed in the master bedroom.

"Amitav, the dinner is served for both of you. Please have it once you are done with the drinks," she said, which Amitav heard inattentively.

"Saroja, please take this glass of cola. I am done with it now," Mustafa said.

She picked up the two glasses of cola and went into another bedroom adjacent to the guest washroom. Since the dinner was already served, she had asked the guest house maid to leave for the night.

She first took out her night gown to change into and after changing, laid back in bed with the quilt over her and sipped from both the glasses of cola while watching TV for some time. She fell asleep without turning off the TV or the lights.

Early in the morning, between 3 and 3.30 AM, 18th December, Saroja was fast sleep, but she wasn't in her night gown anymore. It was dark all around and the winter morning had grown chilly. As Saroja turned to one side, her hand fell on a hairy chest. The touch drew her closer till her nipples were rubbing against the hairy chest. She was aroused. The sensational touch for both the bodies lead to an uncontrolled and passionate love-making. She had never experienced such passionate love since Kabir's demise. From her lips to her neck, her curves, nipples, belly, and then the final destination, she was kissed everywhere. With those powerful strokes in the moments of early morning, she felt like she was on the moon.

After almost an hour and a half, when she woke up around 5 AM, she felt some pain inside her. 'From where had Amitav got such energy last night?' she thought. As she removed the quilt from over herself, she found herself naked, and to her right lay Mustafa Kabir without any clothes on. She screamed. Mustafa got up in haste and was surprised to find himself undressed in Saroja's bed. Saroja had hurriedly put on her night gown in the meantime. She ran out of the room and headed straight to see Ria who was lying asleep on her bed. She ran out shouting, "AMITAV! Where are you?" and found him lying on the sofa in the hall, the same place where he had been drinking the previous night. Amitav got up due to all the noise of screaming and shouting, only to see Saroja standing in front of him in her night gown and crying. Mustafa, who had now put his clothes on, came running after her.

Amitav understood the situation. Mustafa pleaded that it wasn't an intentional act, but had happened unknowingly. He explained, "I felt very heavy after drinking the cola last night. I guess there was wine mixed in it, so I must have gotten high. I went to the washroom when you finished your drink. While in the washroom, I heard the sound of T.V. coming from the adjacent room. When I entered there, I saw that the T.V. was on, which I switched off and was only turning around to come out when I saw Saroja lying in bed in her night gown. Her chest was quite exposed and her quilt had fallen off the side of the bed. I picked up the quilt to put on her, but while putting on the quilt, I looked at her body from up close and lost control. I then remember pulling her gown off, switching off the lights, locking the door and having sex with her, once at midnight while she was sleep, and then again in the wee hours of the morning.

Saroja was shocked and realized that she too had had that cola the previous night and had probably gotten high too. She hadn't felt all that happen to her. 'Perhaps in an unconscious state of mind, I thought that it was Amitav who was making love to me,' she thought. Mustafa couldn't look Saroja in her eyes and his head was hung low in embarrassment. Amitav knew that he was the culprit for having mixed wine in the Cola. It didn't take much time for Saroja to understand too that it was Amitav who had played the mischief, while she had to pay the price. She started crying out of helplessness and frustration.

Amitav didn't know how to react. He felt lost. Mustafa pleaded forgiveness with folded hands. On hearing all the screaming and shouting, Ria had also come out to the hall now. When she saw her mother crying, she ran up to her and hugged her.

"Mamma, don't cry," she said. Saroja patted her with controlled emotion.

"Ria, go to your room," Amitav shouted. Ria got scared and tightly held on to Saroja's legs. Saroja gave Amitav an angry look. Mustafa simply remained standing there.

"Ria, I said go to your room right away," Amitav raised his voice even more. The poor child got so scared that she started crying too. Amitav got up to pounce towards Ria, snatched her from Saroja and beat her up. Saroja lost control and slapped Amitav, while also pulling the weeping Ria away from his hold.

"You dare not touch my daughter," she warned Amitav. He got furious and tried to pull Ria back with force, but could only catch hold of her frock from the back.

"You bitch," he abused. Saroja, on realizing that Ria could be harmed, pushed Amitav back with force. He fell down and banged his head against the brick wall. Ria's frock got torn from behind in this jostle. Saroja hurriedly covered her with her gown and ran into one of the rooms, locking it from the inside. Amitav felt like he had lost consciousness for some time, then got up to sit on the sofa. Mustafa was still watching everything and had begun to feel afraid of the situation.

After some time, Saroja came out of the room with Ria and some packed bags. When she saw Amitav sitting quietly on the sofa and Mustafa still standing there, she declared, "I am leaving you, Amitav. Please don't follow me or try to get me back hereafter. And yes, I am not filing any police complaints against either of you, Mr. Mustafa or Mr.Amitav, for the crimes that you both have committed against me and my daughter."

"I didn't do anything with your daughter," Mustafa said, but she simply stared at him and left, rushing out of the gate. Amitav knew that he had lost her forever. He looked at Mustafa, got up and went inside one of the rooms.

"Sorry, Amitav. Please forgive me if you can," said Mustafa and left the guest house.

When the house maid returned at 8 AM in the morning, Amitav told her, "Madam has left already. I am in no mood to have breakfast. I am leaving too." He then gave her some Rs. 1,000 and instructed her to clean up the apartment and throw away the wine bottles. Soon after, he left the guest house.

Nirbhaya's case dominated the media space and all public platforms for a long time. Saroja landed at the Delhi airport with Ria in the afternoon of 18th December and headed straight to her Hauz Khas house. She picked up all her belongings from there, left a note for Amitav and exited the house before Amitav could reach Hauz Khas.

She called up Kanchan and requested her to arrange for some accommodation for her, if possible, while explaining all that had happened to her. She listened to the plight of Saroja and asked her to come to Lajpat immediately. On her way to Lajpat, Saroja took a contraceptive pill to avoid pregnancy. When Amitav reached Hauz Khas, he read the note that Saroja had left him, then called up his parents and asked if they could suggest him a good lawyer in Delhi for divorce. He also told them all that had transpired between Saroja and him. In some days, he got in touch with a lawyer suggested to him by his parents, called up Saroja and filed consent for a divorce.

Kanchan arranged for a new house for Saroja in vicinity of her own in Lajpat Nagar. The year 2012 was drawing to a close and her parents from Barabanki, along with her brother Kailash and his family, had come to meet Saroja in Delhi. Brijesh learned of it a few days before the new year began when Saroja texted and disclose everything to him. He requested her to forget everything and move on. As the sun set on the eve of the new year, she decided to move on indeed for her daughter Ria's sake.

As the sun rose the next morning, welcoming in the new year, she embraced her life of being a single mother again. She told her parents and siblings that she had no regrets. "When I married Kabir, it was against the wishes of you all, but Kabir was my life, he gave me love, affection and took care of me too. But God took him away from me. I then married Amitav for Ria's sake, thought that I would give life another chance, with the consent of my family too this time, but look what I got in return," she said and hugged her parents. Kailash and Kanchan looked at her with tears in their eyes.

"Don't worry, *gudia.* We are all with you. Come what may, we will always love you," they said. She smiled, while Ria looked at them all.

"Take me in your arms, Mumma," she said innocently. Saroja picked up her adorable daughter in her arms.

By that evening, everyone had left for their respective destinations. Brijesh often called her up on her cellphone and chatted with her. She felt encouraged when Brijesh asked her to concentrate on her preparation for the UPSC interview.

"I need to look for a new job for the time being. If I don't succeed, I will need to work as well," she told Brijesh.

"Relax, things will be fine. Life isn't that harsh," he answered.

"As of now, it is for me, Brijesh. But I will overcome it," she said.

PART 3

Chapter I

Desires

"Is that Amitav speaking?" a gentleman asked from the other side on the cellphone.

"Yes, this is Amitav," he replied.

"Hi, Amitav. This is Zubin Saxena, if you remember. We met at the Goa festival last year. It has almost been six months since then, so I thought I should call you," he said.

"Oh, yeah. I remember," said Amitav.

"Thanks. I hope you have gone through my script. In fact, I am in Delhi right now. Will it be possible for you to meet?" he asked further.

"Frankly speaking, Zubin, I didn't find it worth printing," Amitav lied, as he wanted to avoid further conversation.

"Oh, I see. Anyway, thanks for taking the time to at least read it," Zubin replied and ended the conversation. He then called up Mustafa, but got a disappointing reply from him as well.

"Oh, God! When will I get my chance?" Zubin asked the Almighty, looking up at the sky.

On 16th June, 2013, Saroja's birthday, Kanchan organized a special dinner for her at a five-star hotel on Barakhamba Road. Saroja wasn't in a mood to celebrate, since she had to start preparing for the UPSC preliminaries again, having been unable to get through the interview the previous time. Kanchan, however, wanted to cheer her up and celebrate. Saroja, along with Ria, Kanchan, Arjit and their son were having dinner at the restaurant when Zubin entered the place with some friends, some of them female, and took a corner table. Saroja had noticed him, but he didn't.

They finished dinner and were about to leave, when Saroja excused herself to go to the restroom. As she crossed the room, to go to the restroom area, she looked at Zubin again, but he was busy having dinner with his friends.

"Mumma,"shouted Ria just then and came running after Saroja when she was just about to enter the restroom. When Zubin saw the small child running towards the restroom, his eyes followed and came to rest on the lady whom this child had called 'Mumma'. He tried to recollect where he had seen her before, while Saroja pretended that she hadn't seen him and simply took Ria inside the restroom with her. Zubin fixed a constant glance in the direction of the restroom, and spotted the same lady with girl child again while they were emerging out. Scratching his head, he wondered, “I have surely seen her before, but I can’t remember where.”

Saroja came back to Kanchan’s table. They paid their bill and got ready to leave the place. As she was exiting the restaurant, she turned around and saw Zubin looking straight at her, perhaps trying to recollect where he had seen her before. Out of the exit gate, they got in the car waiting for them at the patio and zoomed out.

Zubin ran towards the exit gate, shouting, “Saroja ma’am!” His friends were surprised to see him running and calling after a woman like that, not knowing that he had recollected her name with a great effort.

At the exit gate, Zubin saw the car zooming away, while he stood helplessly in the drive way. “Do you know the car’s number which just went out?” he asked one of the security personnel.

“No, sir,” came his prompt reply.

Zubin turned around and returned to his seat.

“What happened, Zubin? Who did you follow out?” asked one of his female friends.

“No, it’s nothing,” he answered.

“Then why did you run out, shouting *Saroja*?” asked the same friend, but he kept quiet. “Tell me, who is she?” she enquired.

"I met her at a literary festival last year in Goa. She had come there with her husband, a publisher. I remember giving her my script there, so thought of asking her about it," he explained.

"Oh, Zubin. Don't give me that shit. I know you wouldn't run after some body for just your script," said another male friend.

"Guys, I told you the truth. The rest is up to you to speculate," Zubin answered. "But yes, I am mesmerised by her. She is amazing," he said further.

Back home, Saroja was lying in her bed at night, staring at the ceiling fan. Ria was fast asleep on another bed beside her. Her menstrual cycle has just gotten over a week before and she was unable to sleep. Feeling restless, she got up and started searching for Zubin's script, which she eventually found in the almirah. She started reading it. The story was just as fascinating and engaging as she had found it before. She didn't realize when she fell asleep while reading it.

It was early in the morning that she dreamt about a man cuddling her. He slowly removed her night gown and kissed her breasts and lips. The mere touch of his body gave her pleasure. He went on to kiss her all over, then rode her with powerful strokes. "Aah!" she murmured, while still sleeping. She was aroused even in deep slumber. She saw a young handsome and fair man with curly hair and a bare hairy chest riding her and giving her pleasure.

While he was kissing her lips, her cheeks and her eyes, she recognised the face as Zubin's.

In a flash, her eyes flew open and she looked around to find herself alone. She got up hurriedly, rushed to the washroom, threw her gown to one side and stood beneath the shower. Ria was still fast sleep back in the bedroom. Upon finishing with the shower, she put her night gown back on and entered back into the bedroom. She was all wet, her hair left loose, as she came to stand below the ceiling fan. Looking at the clock hanging on the front wall, she saw that it was 6 AM already. She opened the window of her room to see some cloudy shadows across the early morning sky, heralding the arrival of monsoon in Delhi. She turned around and went to wake her daughter up.

"Riaaa, please get up, dear. You need to be ready before the school bus comes," she said. In another hour's time, she got her daughter ready to go to school.

Once Ria left for school, she kept on thinking about the dream that she had had the night before. She considered sharing it with Kanchan, but then changed her mind. The maid was to arrive soon for the daily cleaning and lunch preparation. Saroja had no job still, besides some consulting assignments regarding the editing of a few magazines, which she had got through Brijesh's recommendations. She spent her time completing those and applying for new jobs till afternoon. This was her routine.

Once Ria got back, she would feed her and help complete her homework till evening, then play with her for some time. Later in the evening, she would devote her time to preparing for the UPSC preliminary exams, while the maid looked after the dinner preparations.

For the last few months, since the Goa incident, Kailash had been transferring sufficient money to his *gudia*'s account each month for her to take care of her expenses. Though she didn't want it, her adoring brother didn't listen to her.

Still engrossed with the dream that she had had the night before, she didn't realized when Ria came back home.

"Mumma, I am hungry," she said as soon as she entered the house. Saroja picked her up, kissed her cheeks and fed her. Taking a deep breath, she looked at Ria and smiled, assuring herself that Ria was her priority and that she had to fulfil her responsibility towards her at any cost. Her desires, sexuality, romance, need for companionship, etc., were all irrelevant when it came to Ria's future, and no matter what hurdles she faced, she had to deal with them all to maintain her focus on her priority.

Whether it was love or just infatuation with Zubin, she asked herself constantly. Later one evening, when she was through with her UPSC preparation for the day and had wrapped up her dinner with Ria, she put her to sleep and picked up Zubin's script again. She finished it in one sitting this time, even though it was early in the morning when she was finally done. She looked at Ria who was in deep sleep, and then went to bed herself to have a nice dream-less sleep.

Chapter 2

Love Again

Almost three years went by, but Saroja could not find full-time employment still. She got many consulting assignments involving editing for a few magazines, but it became difficult for her to manage all her household expenses and growing needs with the money she earned. Her aged father tried his best to contribute some amount to her from his pension, and Kailash would diligently transfer money to Saroja's account every month, yet even all this wasn't sufficient to take care of everything, including her house rent, Ria's school fees, her daily expenses, etc. Saroja could hardly make any savings by herself.

Realizing the difficulties faced by her daughter, Mr. Mishra sold away his house at Varanasi. Adding to it some extra funds which he had managed through his savings, he gifted Saroja a new house at Mayur Vihar Phase 1 in east Delhi, adjacent to Noida. Saroja was reluctant to receive it, but Mr. Mishra insisted, "If I had gotten you married, I would anyway have spent that amount on your wedding. Your siblings have approved it, don't worry."On her mother's request and insistence, they move in with her at the the new house in Mayur Vihar by the end of 2015.

As luck would have it, she soon received an offer from the SPN group of companies based out of Noida sector 18, for the post of an Editor of their in-house magazine. After three long years, she was finally employed with a decent salary. She continued her preparation for UPSC even while working, and did some freelance editing assignments as well. She requested her brother not to transfer her money anymore, and assured him that if she required any help, she would not hesitate to ask him.

Brijesh kept in touch with Saroja through text messages and WhatsApp. They remained best friends as usual. Her life had begun to feel quite smooth again with her parents and Ria. Kanchan often visited her with Arjit and their son. Saroja was regaining her confidence with the support of her loved ones and a special friend like Brijesh. Unfortunately, she could not clear her exams again that year. When the results were declared on 31st May, 2016, she told Brijesh over a call, "I won't give this exam anymore."

"Take a break for a year, then give it a last chance," he insisted.

"Let me see," she replied and decided not to fill the form for the 2016 exam.

*****

As November'16 began, Zubin receive call on his cell phone.

"Is this Mr. Zubin speaking?" the caller asked from the other side.

"Yes, this is Zubin," he answered.

"Mr. Zubin, this is Neha Walia, Secretary to Sanjiv Prakash Nanda, Chairman of the SPN group of companies. I am calling in reference to your profile which we received through our portal for a consulting assignment regarding our upcoming venture on the digital platform–*SPN News*. Would you be interested in meeting with our Chairman this Monday?"

"Well madam, I am away in Nainital at the moment. Would it be convenient if I come and meet him on Friday instead?" he asked.

"Let me check if the Chairman is available that day. Please hold on," she answered, then resumed after about five minutes, "Mr. Zubin, are you there?"

"Yes madam, I am here."

"Alright, Friday, the 11th of November, works for us. Please drop by our office in the evening at 6 PM. I will email you a confirmation with the rest of the details as well," she said.

"Thanks, I will be there," replied Zubin.

Ever so punctual by nature, Zubin reached the SPN office in sector-18, Noida, at the exact time given. He walked up to the reception and asked for Neha Walia. She came to the reception and gave Zubin a form to fill up, as required by the HR policy. In the meantime, she promised to arrange his meeting with the group's Chairman.

"Madam, this is a waste of time and a useless repetition of work. All my details are given on my profile already. Why am I required to fill up this form again?" he said and refused to fill up the form.

"Alright, have a seat then. Would you like to have some coffee or tea?" she asked politely.

"No thanks, just water please," he answered.

Neha ordered the office boy to get him a glass of water and left, requesting Zubin to wait for ten minutes. Zubin waited for the next hour, wondering when those ten minutes would get over and he would be called for a meeting. Receiving no response for so long, he asked the receptionist to remind Neha madam about him. The operator at the reception did so, then told him, "Madam has asked you to wait for another ten minutes," then asked him for coffee or tea again, which Zubin declined again.

It was almost 8:30 PM and Zubin was still waiting to be called in for the meeting. He finally got irritated and left the office, informing at the reception that he couldn't wait any longer. He was on his way back home, which was in Vasundhara Enclave, and had reached the Mayur Vihar Metro Station, when he received a call on his cellphone. It was Neha Walia. "I am extremely sorry, the Chairman got tied up in another assignment, so he could not meet you today," she informed him and requested him to come back on Monday, 14th November, at 11 AM in the morning. Since it was Gurunanak Jayanti that day, Zubin requested her to reschedule it for that evening. She agreed to it and asked him to come at 6PM.

His meeting with the Chairman went extremely well and he was offered a Consulting Editor's job for their portal, *SPN News*. Though Zubin had wanted to be an author all his life, his scripts we're not getting accepted by any publishers, and he was in dire need of a regular income to manage his daily expenses. He was asked to join the group from December the 1st. Zubin wasn't aware that Saroja was also associated with the SPN group till he joined them on 1st December that year. It was when Neha Walia asked the HR department to introduce Zubin to the other SPN employees, that he got to meet Saroja and the other employees. He remembered her this time, but pretended otherwise. She knew that he was trying to feign ignorance. Zubin would occasionally interact with her over some editorial issues, while she would also engage with him, but only over work-related assignments.

In March 2017, Brijesh called up Saroja and informed her that the UPSC exam dates had been declared. He insisted that she give it a last try, since she still had two attempts left. "You may leave it for good if you don't clear it this time," he told her.

"I know, Brijesh. I will give it for the last time this year. Ria is turning ten this year. I guess, I should give a last attempt for Ria's sake."

She informed her parents and siblings of the same, who were more than willing and supportive of her decision. She filled up the online form and got ready to enter the preparation mode, while simultaneously attending office and taking care of Ria and her parents. She was encouraged by Kailash and Ankita through Facebook and WhatsApp. The couple had another child that year, a baby girl this time on April 4th. They often shared her pictures with Saroja on Facebook, to which she always replied with words of affection and blessings. Kanchan and Arjit were happy with their only son, though they adored Ria as if she was their own daughter. This time again, Saroja got through her preliminary exams, held in June'17, and sat for the mains in October, then waited eagerly for the results.

As days progressed, Neha Walia became quite friendly with Zubin. Being the Chairman's Secretary, she claimed to hold a position of high importance and power. The SPN employees did not dare to undermine her self-proclaimed position either. In fact, it was only a matter of convenience and a win-win situation for all of them, except Zubin and Saroja. The two of them didn't really care for who she was.

Neha was separated from her spouse and was a single mother to a four-year-old daughter, Ridhi. She stayed with her parents and a younger brother. Zubin was married himself at the time he joined the SPN group, but he often met Neha and they developed a special bond between them.

Neha started managing Zubin's official trips, booked his airline tickets, arranged his travel schedules and meetings with the Chairman, etc. She was just a phone call away for Zubin, and took care of everything for him. They had an amazing chemistry. She would organise parties and specially invite Zubin to them besides her other few selected friends, Saroja being one of them. There was, however, nothing romantic between Neha and Zubin still, until one day on 11th November, 2017, when Zubin was waiting at the airport at midnight for his flight to arrive. He saw Neha online on WhatsApp and texted her, "My flight is delayed. It's so boring."

"Oh...enjoy," she replied.

"What's there to enjoy? My wife is at home," he texted again.

"Oh, I see. No worries. Look for some girlfriend," she replied.

"I have none," he texted, "Will you be my girlfriend?" he casually asked.

"Yes," came her prompt reply and they went on chatting till Zubin boarded his flight. It was all in good fun for Zubin, but Neha had seized the opportunity quite seriously.

She was open for a relationship and started showering expensive gifts on him. In fact, she slowly started to control Zubin's lifestyle, his attires, his haircuts, his looks–everything was decided by her. Zubin began to feel suffocated under her domination, but ladies know how to please their men and Neha was no exception. She gave him her most prized possession and Zubin succumbed to her passion at once. Although, he resisted her demands thereafter and avoided meeting her on some pretext or the other. Saroja learned that Neha had an eye for Zubin, and started to keep a watch on her activity, though unintentionally.

Neha would often pick Zubin after the office hours and take him for a long drive all the way to Pari Chowk. She would then park her car in some corner below a tree near Pari Chowk were there were the least number of people around and then take pleasure in oral sex with him. She would unzip Zubin's pants, put her hand in to grab his private parts and pull it out from his underpants. While sucking on it, she would ask, "When can I have it in me?"

"Do one thing, remove it and keep it with you in your hand bag, then use it whenever you wish to put it in. It will be a real leather vibrator," he would then say sarcastically.

"Baby, I don't need a sex toy when I can have the real one," she would answer.

While all this was going on, Zubin's eyes once met with Saroja's at one of the parties thrown by Neha. She looked a little uncomfortable whenever Neha drew close to Zubin. As days passed, Zubin and Saroja exchanged their cellphone numbers and started texting each other.

In the first week of January, 2018, Zubin noticed Saroja's profile picture on her WhatsApp account and texted her, "Nice DP."

"Thanks for noticing my profile," she replied.

"I have noticed you as well," he texted back.

On January 10th, 2018, the UPSC Mains' result was out and Saroja was happy to learn that she had cleared it. She now had to wait for her interview the next month.

During the same period, Zubin learned at a party at Neha's residence one day that she was in a relationship with the Chairman of SPN group. In fact, he heard that they had decided to get married and settled down in USA once he got free from some legal hurdles on account of alleged financial irregularity and violation related to the acquisition of a Singapore-based media company MX Media, that had been going on for the last fifteen years, despite a battery of lawyers fighting for him. However, they were expecting it to conclude positively over the next few months.

The Chairman of the SPN group was a very colourful man by nature. Only God knew how serious he was for Neha, while she was under the impression that he was committed to her. This was all very strange since she herself was aware that he had many more female companions.

Zubin detached himself from Neha completely and kept ignoring her. At the same time, he continued exchanging WhatsApp and text massages with Saroja. Zubin would often put a few lines from some romantic song as his WhatsApp status and Saroja would promptly revert by completing the next lines of the song. That's how they grew close to each other, while Zubin parted further from Neha. Zubin and Saroja started chatting for hours over every imaginable subject on earth. They also shared a common interest in literature and poetry. Finally, before Valentine's Day that year, they decided to meet outside of office and spend some time together.

"Why don't you publish your novel?" she asked Zubin.

"I am re-writing it," he answered.

"Will you share what you write with me?"

Zubin nodded. From that day onwards, Zubin started sharing all his writings with Saroja. He completed his novel again and was hell bent on getting it published this time, come what may.

Saroja had to appear for her UPSC interview in a week. She felt prepared and wanted to clear it anyhow.

Neha, on the other hand, couldn't take Zubin's continuous disregard for her and started bad-mouthing and taunting him in the presence of Saroja, not realizing that she too had feelings for Zubin and would eventually inform him of everything. Zubin wasn't bothered at all, though, and kept ignoring her completely.

Zubin and Saroja met every day. She shared her entire life story with him, though he disclosed to her only the relevant parts of his life, not filling in all the details of his time spent with Neha. Despite that, he assured her, albeit needlessly, that there wasn't anything between them anymore.

Saroja confessed to him that she loved him, but did not expect anything in return, except for perhaps a little of his time. Zubin just listened to her without a comment. She shared her feeling for Zubin with Brijesh as well, but he reacted in annoyance and advised her to refrain from him.

"You don't know these writers. They have emotions only in their writings. In reality, they are all assholes. Has he ever given you any gifts?" he asked Saroja.

"No, he hasn't," she answered.

"See, that is how they are–emotionless! Don't repeat the same mistake," he continued. But Saroja wasn't one to listen to him and requested him not to tell anyone about this. He promised he wouldn't. Saroja didn't disclose anything about her relationship with Zubin to anyone else either.

One day, in mid-April, 2018, Zubin texted her, "Let's meet in the evening today at 7PM at Hotel Radisson's, Noida."

"Why at Radisson's?" she asked in reply.

"*Arrey*, let's have coffee together."

"Okay," she replied and they met at the Radisson's as planned.

"Zubin, tell me everything about yourself," she requested him when they met.

"I am from Chandigarh, I already told you that back when we met at the Goa Literary Festival. I am the only son of my parents who manage a cold storage business in Chandigarh," started Zubin. "I wanted to be a writer after I graduated from Chandigarh, but then did my post-graduation as well. I wrote my first novel seven years ago and tried to get it published, but I couldn't get any publisher to do it," Zubin continued, while Saroja just listened quietly.

"When I saw you in Goa for the first time in December 2012, it was love at first sight. I wasn't married then. It was just a coincidence when I saw you again at that five-star hotel in Barakhamba on the eve of 16th June, 2013.I ran after you, calling out your name, but you had already left before you could hear it," Zubin went on saying. Saroja listened to him patiently while recollecting that evening.

"My novel wasn't getting any response even after so many years, I was not earning, I had no job and still shamelessly begged for money from my parents. I had no choice then but to succumb to their pressure and agreed to get married to their choice of a girl in December 2014. I must tell you, I had my share of pleasure with a female colleague before getting married, but it was only a casual thing. She was there with me the day I ran after you at that five star hotel in Barakhamba," Zubin said in one breath. Saroja remained quiet still, recollecting the image of that female companion who had accompanied Zubin that evening. "My better-half is an event manager and travels a lot for her job. I often get lonely in her absence, which is perhaps why I grew close to Neha Walia, but trust me, I never loved her. She was just a very close friend," he concluded. Saroja sipped from a glass of water, since their coffee had turned cold while they were engrossed in this conversation.

Somehow, Saroja felt that Zubin wasn't telling her the complete truth, but she confessed that she loved him regardless. As they say, the desire for sex is the most powerful of human desires, since the desire for sexual expression is natural and comes from within. Physical desire cannot be ignored, especially when you are in love. Their souls met that night and they enjoyed the pleasure that they gave each other at the Radisson's after coffee. She had informed her parents to take care of Ria, as she had an assignment to complete urgently and couldn't return home until the next day.

The next morning, she informed Brijesh of all this. He didn't react, but simply said, "It's your life, Saroja. I won't break my promise, rest assured."A few days after this, she got an invitation from Brijesh to attend his wedding. He was finally getting married to the daughter of a local M.L.A from Unnao, and the wedding had been fixed for 29th April, 2018, at Barabanki.

Neha continued with her tactics to impress Zubin, but he wasn't moved. Saroja could see the desperation in her. When she confronted her one day, she learned that Neha had been more than a close friend to Zubin, and that she had also had her share of physical pleasure with him. Neha was also angry when she learned about Zubin and Saroja. Both of them then confronted Zubin while he was away in Mumbai on an official assignment. He didn't bother to give any clarifications to Neha, but sorted everything out with Saroja immediately.

What Saroja had known was indeed only half the truth. Zubin passionately told her the entire true in a meeting with her at a Starbucks, after his return from Mumbai. He revealed to her how traumatised he had been due to her persistent demanding, her dominating behavior, and a continuous habit of showing-off. Saroja looked into his eyes while sipping coffee, then got up and hugged him tightly

"Since Kabir, I have found true love only in you, and I love you without any expectations. I have seen a lot in life in such a short time. I have been through hell! You were right, it was love at first sight for me too when I met you for the first time in Goa, but I was married then and didn't wanted to break my family for Ria's sake. I avoided you in an attempt to erase all my feeling for you. I avoided meeting you that evening at the Barakhamba hotel, thinking that it wouldn't work between us anyway, since I was trying to recover from Amitav's issue at that time. I never wanted to meet you, but destiny brought you to me again. I have not hidden anything from you. I only wished for you to tell me everything before," she replied in the same strain of passion, in a single breath.

"You know, Saroja, I never asked you about the men in your life. I am not concerned with your past. I agree that you have told me everything about Kabir and Amitav, but" Zubin trailed off.

"But what, Zubin?" she asked with stress, looking into his eyes.

"You didn't tell me anything about Mustafa Kabir. I am not interested in that either, it is just that I learned of it when I met Jaideep Pais, the lawyer whom Amitav had hired for your divorce. Jaideep is my friend from school. Amitav told him everything that happened before filing for divorce," Zubin told her, looking straight at her.

"Then you should know, Zubin, that it was just a mischief by Amitav, which I paid a huge price for. I knew Mustafa liked me, but I wasn't interested in him. He always respected my feelings too. Had Amitav not played this mischief with us, he wouldn't have dared to even touch my body," she said and started weeping upon recollecting the trauma she had gone through that fateful night in December, 2012. Zubin hugged her and tried to comfort her. When she was pacified after some time, they left the coffee shop.

On 27th April, 2018, the UPSC 2017 exam results were finally out. After five tiresome attempts, she had succeeded at last. She informed whomever she knew of this. Congratulatory massages poured in from every one, right from Brijesh, Zubin, her siblings, her parents, Mr. and Mrs. Singh and many others. Mr. and Mrs. Mishra travelled with Saroja and Ria to spend the next two days at Barabanki to attend Brijesh's wedding. Kanchan and Kailash wished him through Facebook. Mr. and Mrs. Singh were finally pleased to see their only son getting married.

Zubin, having finished his novel finally, got a publisher to publish it too. He had submitted the edited script to a Mumbai-based publisher during the last week of April, and informed Saroja that it had gotten accepted when she met him after her return from Barabanki.

"What's next?" she asked him.

"I will start my next book on your life."

"Really?" she asked.

"Yes, for sure. And if things go as planned, I will give you the manuscript to read on your birthday, June 16th, before forwarding it to the publisher," he replied.

"Sounds good," she answered with a twinkle in her eyes.

This time, she hosted a big party to celebrate her daughter's birthday on 27th May, with Kanchan's and her own family. A few days later, she received a WhatsApp text from Amitav, informing her of his father's demise on 2nd June in Siliguri, West Bengal. She took the first flight available to reach Siliguri via Calcutta, en route Bagdogra.

At 8 AM in the morning, a palatial bungalow in the city of Siliguri hosted many guest who had come to pay their homage to the departed soul of Mr.Sanyal, Amitav's father. His body was wrapped in a white cotton cloth. Saroja's eyes met with Amitav's mother's as she entered. Saroja rushed to touch her feet and take her blessings. Amitav followed behind his mother and greeted her with folded hands. She looked at him, then moved ahead to where the body of Sr. Mr. Sanyal was placed. She bent down to touch her feet too.

When she straightened up, she saw Mustafa Kabir standing in a corner. The look of his person had changed entirely. He had grown out a beard, but without a moustache. He was dressed like a Maulvi or Maulana. Ignoring him, she looked around the verandah. Her gaze came to rest at a tree planted to her left, within the bungalow's premises. It was a parijaat tree. It had very few flowers remaining on its branches, since most of them had bloomed and dropped down upon the touch of the first rays of the sun which had just come out from behind a monsoon cloud.

Perhaps they wanted to pay their homage to the departed soul as well. After the funeral ceremonies were over, Mustafa came back to the Bungalow, met Amitav briefly, then came forward to meet Saroja.

"I am here only to ask for your forgiveness. I know I have committed a sin, though unknowingly, and am now paying the price for it as well. I am all alone. My parents are resting in peace, and my own body awaits the graveyard now. I am suffering from blood cancer, and I won't last long. I have left my occupation and spend all my time in religious activities. I beg you to forgive me. I knew you'd be here the moment I saw Amitav's text, so I took the opportunity to meet you and seek your forgiveness personally," Mustafa pleaded with folded hands.

"I have forgiven you, Mustafa. I have no ill feelings towards you," she said.

"Will you forgive my son too?" Amitav's mother approached Saroja and pleaded.

She hugged the old lady and said while looking at Amitav, "I have forgiven you too, Amitav." Both the women then held each other and cried.

Before leaving the next morning, she informed them about her success in the UPSC exams. They were all pleased to know it and blessed her. She learned later that Amitav had permanently shifted to Siliguri. Mustafa got admitted to a cancer hospital in Delhi within a week of his return, but died soon after. As promised, Zubin completed his novel based on her life and gave her a hardcopy of the script on her birthday. They were both back at the Starbucks in Noida, sipping on their favourite coffees together.

"You know, Zubin, even though I love you, I feel that your wife needs you more than I do. From Saroja Mishra, I went on to become Saroja Prajapati, then Saroja Sanyal, and now I am just Saroja...Saroja Kumari, and this is my journey hereafter. I will travel ahead on the road of my life with only Ria. I have quit the SPN Group job and am heading to Mussoorie for my training soon. I thought that we'd have coffee together today for old time's sake."

Zubin smiles at her as they get up after their last sip, and they give each other a long hug. "Please take care of yourself," she said with tears in her eyes.

"You too," he answered and they departed from the venue.

Saroja soon started her training at Mussoorie, while Ria was taken care of by her parents back in Mayur Vihar. She visited Delhi now and then to meet them and Kanchan's family. Kailash remained in Singapore with his family. Zubin quit SPN News soon after and joined a publishing house in Delhi as an Editor. He remained in touch with Saroja through text massages. Brijesh went on to become a Collector in the city of Benaras, where he lived with his wife and parents. He too remained in touch with Saroja through text massages.

In a month thereafter, Saroja received a courier in her name at the Mussoorie Training Centre. She opened it to find inside a book titled *'Saroja'*, authored by Zubin Saxena. On the first page, he had written in his handwriting, '*With love, yours Zubin*' with his signature beneath it.